The Adventures of
Helicopter Jim

Stones of the Months
Part 3

Sheldon R. Lacsina

The Adventures of Helicopter Jim
Stones of the Months-Part 3
Copyright © 2020 by Sheldon R. Lacsina

All rights reserved. No part of this book may be reproduced or transmitted in any form or by any means without written permission from the author.

ISBN 9798597156910

Dedication

Thank you Jesus for loving the world the way You do.

Thank you Heidi for your unbelievable support, encouragement, and as always...inspiration!

Thank you Justin, Raine, and my grandchildren, Jayden, Landen, and Oakley, for adding joy to my life!

Thank you Jordan for always encouraging me and for being adventurous.

Thank you to all of you who have brought these adventures to life through your creative voices and ongoing imagination.

What are the Adventures of Helicopter Jim?

Helicopter Jim is a preteen who has been given an assignment to locate "The Stones of the Months" which when returned to its proper place, will restore peace and order to the entire universe.

It is short adventure stories. It could be read before bedtime, on car trips (make sure the driver is not the reader…thought I'd throw that in as a disclaimer just in case), for class time, camping trips, or whenever you think best. After each story ends, it continues the next day and not until then. That's what makes it adventurous, you need to hang on until...

...*the next Adventure of Helicopter Jim.*

Email: theadventuresofhelicopterjim@gmail.com

Social Networks:
Twitter: @AHJthebook
Facebook: Helicopter Jim
YouTube: The Adventures of Helicopter Jim
Blog: theadventuresofhelicopterjim.blogspot.com
http://www.spreaker.com/user/ahjthebook
http://soundcloud.com/ahjthebook

Preface

As I finished parts one and two, my excitement for part three increased...although I'm the author, I too can't wait to see what will happen next. Even though I have an idea of what's coming up on the next adventure, I too am bummed when I hear those heart crushing words...
AND THAT WILL BE THE NEXT ADVENTURE OF HELICOPTER JIM!!!

YOU MUST READ THESE INSTRUCTIONS!!!

1. Be involved in the story.
2. Each character has its own voice, you must make one for them...and work very hard at remembering the VOICE or it'll change as you go...and that won't go so well for you with the kids...believe me, they'll notice!
3. There are certain sound effects that are in (parenthesis) that you will need to make. When it says, (EXPLOSION) you need to make the sound of an explosion, not say the word EXPLOSION.
4. Under no circumstances should you proceed to the next adventure on the same day, it is critical to wait for the next day to read the next adventure. This will spark imagination and creativity in the listener.
5. You must read with emotion, like you're telling a story, not reading a book. Excitement, drama, sadness, whispering, etc., is what makes HJ different than any other reading.
6. HAVE FUN reading!

For a sample on how to read the adventures, visit any of our Social Network media sites.

IF YOU READ PARTS 1 & 2 AND THE INSTRUCTIONS ON PAGE 6, PROCEED...IF YOU HAVE NOT...YOU MUST READ PARTS 1 & 2, AND THE INSTRUCTIONS BEFORE STARTING.

Adventure 101

On the last adventure of Helicopter Jim, Mikhail, Princess Eva, Queen Avehi, Advan and Targy, are making their way out of the maze of tunnels. Mikhail and Princess Eva are having a tough time staying connected to (HELICOPTER NAME) because they are deeply underground.

As they're heading out of this maze of tunnels, they're going left and right, up and down, up some ladders, down some stairs. They're going down tunnel after tunnel and they cannot find their way out. And they're trying to figure out how to get out. Just then, Mikhail had a thought...

MIKHAIL: "Wait a minute, what if we were to continue to go up...just look for areas that we can go up. We have access to (HELICOPTER NAME) but there's no signal right now. We can't- we can't connect. That must mean we're deep below the surface."

So they try their very best to find their way out. As they turn down this one tunnel, all of a sudden, they feel this darkness, almost like an evil creature is near them.

QUEEN AVEHI: "Stop!"

AND NOW WE BEGIN THE ADVENTURES OF

HELICOPTER JIM!

Advan and Targy, they sense something, and so the both of them, both Advan and Targy slowly make their way down the tunnel. As they're heading down this tunnel, the Queen instructs Mikhail and the Princess...

QUEEN AVEHI: "Stay here."

So Mikhail and Princess Eva stay in that spot while Advan and Targy continue down this long tunnel. As they're going down this tunnel, there are places that they can go to, they can go to the left or they can go to the right. And there are various openings down this tunnel. They just don't know which way to go... left or right, yet they still sense something evil down there.

As they continue to go down this tunnel, all of a sudden, they hear a loud roar. Advan and Targy stop. They look at each other, and they look at the Queen.

ADVAN: "We know that roar. That... is Wyder, servant to Dayor."

QUEEN AVEHI: "Why would Wyder be here? Why-why-why would Dayor send one of his subjects here?"

ADVAN: "I do not know, but Ma'am, for your safety, you need to stay here while Targy and I take on Wyder."

So the Queen stayed back, while Advan and Targy head down the tunnel and look for Wyder.

The Queen goes back to Mikhail and Princess Eva to let them know what is about to happen.

QUEEN AVEHI: "Advan and Targy believe that one of

Dayor's creatures is down here. I don't know why Dayor would send one of his creatures down here, but Advan and Targy are going to have to fight Wyder in order for us to get out of here."

As Advan and Targy continue down the tunnel, they sense that Wyder is nearby.

And sure enough, Wyder is right around the corner. As Advan and Targy come around the corner they are faced with Wyder.

Wyder is twice as big as both Advan and Targy put together. Wyder is very strong and quick and smart, but Advan and Targy are also smart. Advan and Targy attack Wyder (SWOOSH GSHHH!). They split up, attack his feet and his knees (KGSHHH!). Wyder moves away very quickly (FEWSH!). And even though Advan and Targy are quick, it seems like Wyder is even quicker. They fight for so long that they are all wounded and tired.

WYDER: (BREATHING HEAVILY) "You will not defeat me. I will defeat you. Give up or suffer the consequences!"

TARGY: (BREATHING HEAVILY) "We will never give up. You give up or you will suffer the consequences!"

Wyder attacked Advan and Targy (BOOOSHH!). They fought for many more hours. Finally, Advan jumps on Wyder's back, takes a hold of his neck and holds him there while Targy gives Wyder a blow to his midsection (BWAAH!). And finally Wyder is knocked out. Advan and Targy are so tired that they cannot even move.

The Queen notices that there is no more movement. Nor can she hear them fighting anymore. And so she heads towards where they were fighting and she sees Advan and Targy on the ground, tired and wounded... Wyder is also tired and wounded, and knocked out. The Queen comes up to Advan and Targy, touches them and heals them. Advan and Targy slowly get up...

ADVAN: "Thank you, your Majesty."

QUEEN AVEHI: "Take him prisoner. We're going to take Wyder with us."

So they continue to head out of the tunnels, trying to find their way out. They go up some stairs and as they do, Mikhail and the Princess regain signal with (HELICOPTER NAME).

(STATIC RADIO SOUND F/X)

HELICOPTER: "There you are. I lost you some time ago. Are you okay?"

MIKHAIL: "We are doing fine. We just went through some battles. Well, not we, as in the Princess and I...more like them...Advan and Targy. They were in a battle with Wyder"

HELICOPTER: "I'm glad everyone is doing okay."

MIKHAIL: "Everyone except for Wyder."

HELICOPTER: "Wyder! He's one of Dayor's loyal subjects."

MIKHAIL: "That is correct (HELICOPTER NAME). Okay...now how do we get out of here?"

So (HELICOPTER NAME) guides them out of the tunnels and meets them at the exit point. Avan and Targy are taking the Queen back to her city. Mikhail and the Princess jump into (HELICOPTER NAME), and they follow the Queen to Amethyst City.

QUEEN AVEHI: "Quick! We must get back to Amethyst City!"

AND THAT WILL BE THE NEXT ADVENTURE OF HELICOPTER JIM.

Adventure 102

On the last adventure of Helicopter Jim, Mikhail, Princess Eva, Queen Avehi, Advan and Targy needed to find their way out of the underground maze of tunnels. All of a sudden, they heard a loud roar! It was Wyder, one of Dayor's most loyal subjects.

Advan and Targy battle with Wyder, and eventually knock him out, defeating him.

QUEEN AVEHI: "Take him prisoner. We're going to take Wyder with us."

So they continue to head out of the tunnels, trying to find their way out. They go up some stairs and as they do, Mikhail and the Princess regain signal with (HELICOPTER NAME).

(STATIC RADIO SOUND F/X)

HELICOPTER: "There you are. I lost you some time ago. Are you okay?"

MIKHAIL: "We are doing fine. We just went through some battles. Well, not we, as in the Princess and I...more like them...Advan and Targy. They were in a battle with Wyder"

HELICOPTER: "I'm glad everyone is doing okay."

MIKHAIL: "Everyone except for Wyder."

HELICOPTER: "Wyder! He's one of Dayor's loyal subjects."

MIKHAIL: "That is correct (HELICOPTER NAME)...and this is Advan and Targy...they're with the Queen... Okay...now how do we get out of here?"

So (HELICOPTER NAME) guides them out of the tunnels

and meets them at the exit point. Avan and Targy are taking the Queen back to her city. Mikhail and the Princess jump into (HELICOPTER NAME), and they follow the Queen to Amethyst City.

QUEEN AVEHI: "Quick! We must get back to Amethyst City!"

AND NOW WE BEGIN THE ADVENTURES OF HELICOPTER JIM!

Meanwhile, Scott and Mr. Cape were resting with the Aadryans, who were still in a deep sleep. Mr. Cape was wondering if they should figure out another way to find Jim because it was taking so long for Mikhail and the Princess to give any word of where they were.

SCOTT: "What are you thinking? I can see you're thinking about something."

MR. CAPE: "I was thinking maybe we should try to figure out another way to get to Jim or at least to try to find where the Princess and Mikhail are."

SCOTT: "Where would we go? What would we even think of or what can we possibly do? We're in the middle of this ocean, and all we have here are sleeping Aadryans? They're no use to us. They can't even help us right now. They're in this deep sleep. I don't even know what's happening with them."

MR. CAPE: "I was thinking about why they would be in such a deep sleep because they have a lot of energy so why would they be in a deep sleep?"

As they were thinking of how to find Helicopter Jim and the

rest of the team, all of a sudden, the Aadryans, one by one, began to slowly wake up.

SCOTT: "Hey, hey, hey, hey, I felt something. This Aadryan moved. I felt it...I felt it move."

MR. CAPE: "Oh, they're getting up. I can see them. They're waking up, so maybe this is our opportunity to see if we can use the Aadryans."

Mr. Cape and Scott were on the Aadryans. They both had one Aadryan each and they were hanging on to the fin of the Aadryan. The Aadryans woke up and seemed like they were more alert than before. As Scott and Mr. Cape were trying to figure a way to get to Helicopter Jim and to see if they could meet up with the rest of the team, all of a sudden, the Aadryans bolted. (DEWFF!)

Mr. Cape and Scott is blazing through the ocean. (ELECTRICAL SOUND F/X) They are hanging on so tight and the next thing they knew, is they are exactly in the same area where (HELICOPTER NAME), Mikhail, Princess Eva, Queen Avehi, Advan, and Targy are.

MR. CAPE: "I see them up ahead!"

SCOTT: "I see them too. That was crazy! Hey...what are the other things? Who is that? What are those big creatures?"

MR. CAPE: "I don't know, but I'm sure we'll find out. I hope everything is okay."

As they got closer, (HELICOPTER NAME) let Mikhail and Princess Eva know that Mr. Cape and Scott were right behind them.

MIKHAIL: "Hey, Mr. Cape, how are you?"

MR. CAPE: "We're doing great! We're doing okay. We're just thankful that the Aadryans woke up. How many days were you guys gone?"

MIKHAIL: "I'm not sure. I know it was awhile. I lost track of time."

SCOTT: "We're starving. We need some food."

HELICOPTER: "I got you covered. I'll make something for you guys. Would you like nachos or burgers and shakes or some steaks and tater tots..."

SCOTT: "Yes please!"

HELICOPTER: "Yes to what?"

PRINCESS EVA: "I think he wants it all...You're always hungry, Scott."

SCOTT: "No, not always… but this time, I am really hungry. We didn't eat much. We didn't know you guys were going to be gone that long. What have you guys been doing?"

PRINCESS EVA: "We were rescuing someone who we thought was Jim."

MR. CAPE: "You rescued someone? Who did you rescue?"

PRINCESS EVA: "The Queen of Amethyst City, which is where we're heading right now."

SCOTT: "What are those big creatures?"

MIKHAIL: "Those creatures are friends of the Queen."

MR. CAPE: "And that one?"

MIKHAIL: "Oh, that's Wyder, one of the servants of Dayor."

They were approaching Amethyst City, and as they were approaching, they saw…

AND THAT WILL BE THE NEXT ADVENTURE OF HELICOPTER JIM.

Adventure 103

On the last adventure of Helicopter Jim, Scott and Mr. Cape caught up with Mikhail and Princess Eva as they were heading to Amethyst City, along with Queen Avehi, Advan, Targy and Wyder as their prisoner.

SCOTT: "We're starving. We need some food."

HELICOPTER: "I got you covered. I'll make something for you guys. Would you like nachos or burgers and shakes or some steaks and tater tots..."

SCOTT: "Yes please!"

HELICOPTER: "Yes to what?"

PRINCESS EVA: "I think he wants it all...You're always hungry, Scott."

SCOTT: "No, not always... but this time, I am really hungry. We didn't eat much. We didn't know you guys were going to be gone that long. What have you guys been doing?"

PRINCESS EVA: "We were rescuing someone who we thought was Jim."

MR. CAPE: "You rescued someone? Who did you rescue?"

PRINCESS EVA: "The Queen of Amethyst City, which is where we're heading right now."

SCOTT: "What are those big creatures?"

MIKHAIL: "Those creatures are friends of the Queen."

MR. CAPE: "And that one?"

MIKHAIL: "Oh, that's Wyder, one of the servants of Dayor."

They were approaching Amethyst City, and as they were approaching, they saw…

AND NOW WE BEGIN THE ADVENTURES OF HELICOPTER JIM!

As they approached the city they saw... one of the Aadryans still at the entrance point of the palace, of the city.

SCOTT: "Hey, that's the Aadryan Jim was on!"

QUEEN AVEHI: "Yes, these Aadryans know exactly where to go too when it comes to the Chosen One."

MR. CAPE: "Wow, that's incredible! They knew Jim was the Chosen One?"

QUEEN AVEHI: "No, not exactly, they just know who to help when it comes to the Stone of July."

SCOTT: "Do you know about the Stone of July?"

QUEEN AVEHI: "Yes, we do."

SCOTT: "I have a question. What are these things? What do they do... these Aadryans, and why were they sleeping?"

QUEEN AVEHI: "The Aadryans help us with protecting the Stone of July. And although they are very fast, they drain very quickly of energy. When they're sleeping, they're recharging, so that they're able to bolt through these waters and get to places quickly."

They now arrived at the entrance of the city. Advan and Targy put Wyder in chains and in one of the rooms to keep him secure.

MIKHAIL: "What do we do now?"

QUEEN AVEHI: "I am going to my palace because that's where my sister is."

The Queen headed to the palace and sure enough, there was the Queen's sister. Everyone knew that the Queen had returned. What the Queen also recognized was that the city was glowing, brighter than usual.

The Queen greeted her sister...

QUEEN AVEHI: (WITH A STERN VOICE) "You will never hold within your possession the Stone of July. We have been protectors over this Stone for years. We will not let you betray the oath that we made. I will give you two choices. Either you leave and never return, or suffer the consequences if you stay."

PRINCESS ALIYAH: (ARROGANTLY) "My, my, my, why are you so difficult? You know that if we hand the Stone over to Dayor, then he will also protect us."

QUEEN AVEHI: "Protect us from what? From who? Don't be misled by him. He knows that if you are fearful, then he can control you, but if you remain faithful to the oath that we took, then one day the Chosen One will be able to bring peace to the entire universe."

MIKHAIL: "We believe that Jim is the Chosen One."

QUEEN AVEHI: "He's here, isn't he...and he's in the vault right now, isn't he?"

PRINCESS ALIYAH: "I have never doubted your wisdom and your decisions. I will abide by your request, and I will leave freely on my own."

The Queen's sister began to leave, and Scott spoke up...

SCOTT: "Wait, wait a minute, wait a minute, you're going to let your sister go free? What if she comes back later and does something mean?"

The Queen's sister looked at Scott...

PRINCESS ALIYAH: "Who are you, and how dare you come between my sister and I? You have no say, and you have no power. I wouldn't say another word if I were you."

QUEEN AVEHI: "He does have power. His power is being my friend. Whatever you're going to do sister, do it quickly."

The Queen's sister left.

MR. CAPE: "Scott does have a point. You're just going to let her go free?"

QUEEN AVEHI: "Yes, I don't worry about her. She's been like that as long as I can remember. I do know this, that if Helicopter Jim is the Chosen One, then we have a lot of work to do. Follow me... I know where Jim is."

MIKHAIL: "Why is this city so quiet? Where is everyone?"

QUEEN AVEHI: "I'm pretty sure people are in hiding because of my sister. It's okay, don't worry about it. They're okay. Quick, follow me."

While (HELICOPTER NAME) waited at the entrance of the Palace, the Queen took everyone to where the vault was, and all the Queen did is touch the walls, and it became transparent, invisible.

SCOTT: "Jim! Hey, Jim!"

They could see Jim, right in the middle of the room, but Jim couldn't see them.

QUEEN AVEHI: "He cannot hear you...he is trapped in a state of emptiness."

SCOTT: "What! Get him out of there!"

MIKHAIL: "What do we do now?"

AND THAT WILL BE THE NEXT ADVENTURE OF HELICOPTER JIM.

Adventure 104

On the last adventure of Helicopter Jim, Queen Avehi, Mikhail, Scott, Mr. Cape and Princess Eva arrived at Amethyst City and the Queen was able to confront her sister. The Queen gave her sister two options: *Leave and never return, or stay and suffer the consequences.*

The Queen's sister, Aliyah, chose to leave. Queen Avehi knew Jim was in the vault and led everyone there.

While (HELICOPTER NAME) waited at the entrance of the Palace, the Queen took everyone to where the vault was, and all the Queen did is touch the walls, and it became transparent, invisible.

SCOTT: "Jim! Hey, Jim!"

They could see Jim, right in the middle of the room, but Jim couldn't see them.

QUEEN AVEHI: "He cannot hear you...he is trapped in a state of emptiness."

SCOTT: "What! Get him out of there!"

MIKHAIL: "What do we do now?"

AND NOW WE BEGIN THE ADVENTURES OF HELICOPTER JIM!

QUEEN AVEHI: "All I need to do is open the vault, and Helicopter Jim will be able to come out."

SCOTT: "How do you do that? How do you open the vault?"

QUEEN AVEHI: "I will need to release the power of the

walls by sending someone into the same opening Jim was sent through."

SCOTT: "Why the same opening?"

QUEEN AVEHI: "If not, Jim will be stuck in the vault...it's the way the vault is designed...and knowing my sister, she changed the sequence of the doors."

MR. CAPE: "So what will we need to do?"

QUEEN AVEHI: "Someone needs to enter the vault through the right doorway before the walls dim. And if we enter the wrong doorway, both Jim and whoever we send, will be trapped there forever."

SCOTT: "Then send me...I'll go."

PRINCESS EVA: "Scott, no! If you enter the wrong door, you'll be trapped too!"

SCOTT: "Princess, we don't have much time...look, the walls are dimming!"

The walls were almost completely dimmed...

QUEEN AVEHI: "Scott, you will have to go through one of those doors up there...either the top, left, right, or the bottom one...

SCOTT: "Which one do I go through?! Hurry...the walls are almost out!"

QUEEN AVEHI: "No one can choose for you Scott...you must choose."

Scott didn't know what to do...he could see Jim suspended on the other side of the walls...which were almost completely dimmed.

SCOTT: (SPEAKING EMOTIONALLY SOFTLY) "Jim...I don't know which door...and if I choose wrong, we will both be trapped forever...if I choose wrong Jim, I'm so sorry...you've been my best friend all of my life and have always been there for me...I hope I'm able to be here for you. You have always been the Chosen One to me."

Just then Scott chose a door and went through…

AND THAT WILL BE THE NEXT ADVENTURE OF HELICOPTER JIM.

Adventure 105

On the last adventure of Helicopter Jim, Scott, Mr. Cape, Mikhail and the Princess, were led by Queen Avehi to the vault where Jim was trapped. If the walls dimmed completely, the vault would lock Jim in there forever.

Scott needed to choose the right door to go through in order to free Jim. If he chose the wrong door, both he and Jim would be trapped in the vault forever.

The walls were almost completely dimmed...

QUEEN AVEHI: "Scott, you will have to go through one of those doors up there...either the top, left, right, or the bottom one...

SCOTT: "Which one do I go through?! Hurry...the walls are almost out!"

QUEEN AVEHI: "No one can choose for you Scott...you must choose."

Scott didn't know what to do...he could see Jim suspended on the other side of the walls...which were almost completely dimmed.

SCOTT: (SPEAKING EMOTIONALLY SOFTLY) "Jim...I don't know which door...and if I choose wrong, we will both be trapped forever...if I choose wrong Jim, I'm so sorry...you've been my best friend all of my life and have always been there for me...I hope I'm able to be here for you. You have always been the Chosen One to me."

Just then Scott chose a door and went through...

AND NOW WE BEGIN THE ADVENTURES OF HELICOPTER JIM!

The walls dimmed completely. They could no longer see through the walls...it was completely dark in the vault. They could no longer see Jim. There was no glow from the walls.

PRINCESS EVA: "Did it work? Did he choose the right door? What just happened? Where are they?"

QUEEN AVEHI: "If he did make it, he's going to have to bring Jim out from the vault."

It was silent....(PAUSE FOR 3 SECONDS)

All of a sudden, (RUMBLING SOUND) the walls began to shake...and then, to everyone's amazement, the walls began to glow once again. (MAKE A GLOWING SOUND F/X)

MR. CAPE: "There they are! I see them!"

MIKHAIL: "Well done Scott!"

Helicopter Jim and Scott could see everyone from the other side of the vault. Helicopter Jim was relieved. He thought that was the end of his journey.

Scott and Helicopter Jim came out of the vault from the door Scott entered.

HJ: "Mr. Cape, Mikhail, Princess, what happened? What are you doing here? How did you get here? Who are these other people?"

QUEEN AVEHI: "I am Queen Avehi. These two are Advan and Targy. I met your friends and they told me who you were. I believe that you're here for the Stone of July."

HJ: "Wait...you're the Queen?! So who was the other Queen? And what do you know about July?"

QUEEN AVEHI: "She is no Queen, she is my sister, Princess Aliyah. She tricked you to make you think she was the Queen. And as for July...let's just say we have the same goal."

HJ: "Yeah...she definitely tricked me... but I don't know what to do. I don't know where the Stone is or how to retrieve it."

QUEEN AVEHI: "That's the challenge. The challenge is retrieving it. You know when they had us guard each Stone, it wasn't just guarding the Stones. It was making sure that the Chosen One would be the only one who could retrieve it. This is how we guarded the Stone. Every protector is going to guard the Stone differently, but this is how we chose to guard the Stone of July. I suppose you have the Stone of January because, without January, you're not able to retrieve any of the other Stones."

HJ: "Yes, I do. What do I need to do to retrieve the Stone of July?"

TARGY: "You're going to need a lot of strength."

HJ: "Maybe that's why I need the Stone of January. Where do I find the Stone of July? Where is the Stone of July?"

QUEEN AVEHI: "The Stone of July is in the vault."

HJ: "No, it's not in the vault, I was in the vault. You just released me from the vault. It is pitch black, there's nothing in there."

QUEEN AVEHI: "It's in there, you just didn't know how to retrieve it."

HJ: "If I could see it, then I could retrieve it.'"

QUEEN AVEHI: "No, you couldn't because you were filled with fear, weren't you?"

HJ: "How did you know?"

QUEEN AVEHI: "Because that's what my sister does best. She is able to cast fear on people, which paralyzes them, and allows them not to see their full potential and what they're capable of. I can tell you this; when you go back into the vault, you're going to need a lot of strength, not just physical strength, you're going to need strength of the mind. In other words, you're going to need January."

HJ: "Okay, so (DEEP BREATH AND SIGH) what do I do?"

QUEEN AVEHI: "The way we designed the vault to protect the Stone of July is to continuously fight against anyone who tried to take the Stone, so that not just anyone could retrieve the Stone. The only one who can retrieve the Stone, is the Chosen One, because you need January. You will need wisdom and you will need strength. You need strength of the mind and physical strength."

HJ: "Okay, I was in the vault, and I'm not sure where to start...how do I even know what to do?"

QUEEN AVEHI: "When you get in there, use wisdom of the mind, and you'll know what to do, because you don't have any fear now"

The Queen led Helicopter Jim back into the vault. He didn't need to go through the doors that the Queen's sister made him go through.

All the Queen did was touch the walls, and it allowed Helicopter Jim to go right through it. She touched the walls and Helicopter Jim entered the vault. She released her hand from the wall and the rest of the team could not see Jim anymore. They could just see the wall in the palace.

MIKHAIL: "What do we do now? Do we just wait?"

QUEEN AVEHI: "Yes."

PRINCESS EVA: "How long do we wait?"

AND THAT WILL BE THE NEXT ADVENTURE OF HELICOPTER JIM.

Adventure 106

On the last adventure of Helicopter Jim, Scott was able to bring Jim out of the vault because he chose the right door to enter. Helicopter Jim was able to exit the vault and see everyone.

Now, Helicopter Jim needed to go back into the vault to retrieve the Stone of July.

QUEEN AVEHI: "When you get in there, use wisdom of the mind, and you'll know what to do, because you don't have any fear now"

The Queen led Helicopter Jim back into the vault. He didn't need to go through the doors that the Queen's sister made him go through.

All the Queen did was touch the walls, and it allowed Helicopter Jim to go right through it. She touched the walls and Helicopter Jim entered the vault. She released her hand from the wall and the rest of the team could not see Jim anymore. They could just see the wall in the palace.

MIKHAIL: "What do we do now? Do we just wait?"

QUEEN AVEHI: "Yes."

PRINCESS EVA: "How long do we wait?"

AND NOW WE BEGIN THE ADVENTURES OF HELICOPTER JIM!

QUEEN AVEHI: "We wait, Princess, as long as it takes for him to retrieve July."

SCOTT: "Is he going to be okay? Is he going to be safe?

How do we even know he's going to make it? What if he doesn't make it? What if he needs help? Can I go in there? Can I help him? Can I at least be with him?"

QUEEN AVEHI: "No, it doesn't work that way. The vault was created in such a way where only the Chosen One can be in there to retrieve the Stone."

MR. CAPE: "It's okay Scott, Jim will be fine. He has January, he needs to do this on his own."

Helicopter Jim was in the vault, and he found himself once again having to figure out how to retrieve July. This time he wasn't filled with fear, he was filled with hope. He reached into his pouch and took out January. As he held January in his hands, he needed strength of the mind...he needed wisdom.

HJ: (THINKING TO HIMSELF) "In this place, how would I be able to retrieve something I cannot see? If it's totally dark, how can I retrieve what I cannot see? I cannot feel it, and I cannot see it. What do I do?"

As Helicopter Jim was thinking, all of a sudden, he thought of what could possibly be the reason why he cannot see the Stone. What he thought about was the way the Stone is protected...wisdom said that the Stone is in tiny pieces. It is broken apart in its very own structure by each molecule. In other words, the Stone of July is everywhere in the vault.

The only way Helicopter Jim can retrieve the Stone of July is to find a way to bring each molecule of the Stone of July all together in one piece.

He's wondering how to do this, he thinks and thinks, and he

figures...

HJ: "Maybe if I am able to break through the darkness, then maybe something can happen."

He's swimming around and continuously swims around. He looks around and still nothing. Then he remembers what the Queen's sister said. She said if I go through the wall, then I'm not able to come back in. Maybe she said that so that I don't go outside of the walls. She made me fearful of failing if I went through the walls.

Helicopter Jim put January back in his pouch, and he took out August and became invisible. While he was invisible, he was able to go through the wall. Helicopter Jim went through the wall of the palace, and he found himself not outside of the palace, he found himself in another room. A room filled with what looked like amethyst Stones, huge, shiny, purple, sparkly, glass-like looking crystals and gems. Helicopter Jim was in awe...

HJ: "What do I do with this?"

As he looks around, he notices that all of these structures has a certain glow about them. He examined the entire place and notices that there is a certain pattern of how these structures are designed. Helicopter Jim figured out that there is a certain pattern for a reason. He put August back in his pouch, and he took out January and had to think. What he knew is that this structure was designed to be a compactor, which means it was designed to smash things. Helicopter Jim had to figure out a way to get this structure around the vault.

He thought that if he was able to get this structure around the vault, and with enough strength, he would be able to use this structure to crush the vault, and in doing so, bring all of the molecules of the Stone of July together.

Would it be possible? Jim felt that this is the best plan to try…

AND THAT WILL BE THE NEXT ADVENTURE OF HELICOPTER JIM.

Adventure 107

On the last adventure of Helicopter Jim, Jim risked going through the wall and when he did, he found himself in another room. Jim needed to figure out a way to retrieve the Stone of July. He believed the molecules of July were scattered in the vault, and he needed to find a way to bring them all together.

The only problem was, to move and use the structure, would require a lot of physical effort.

HJ: "What do I do with this?"

As he looks around, he notices that all of these structures has a certain glow about them. He examined the entire place and notices that there is a certain pattern of how these structures are designed. Helicopter Jim figured out that there is a certain pattern for a reason. He put August back in his pouch, and he took out January and had to think. What he knew is that this structure was designed to be a compactor, which means it was designed to smash things. Helicopter Jim had to figure out a way to get this structure around the vault.

He thought that if he was able to get this structure around the vault, and with enough strength, he would be able to use this structure to crush the vault, and in doing so, bring all of the molecules of the Stone of July together.

Would it be possible? Jim felt that this is the best plan to try…

AND NOW WE BEGIN THE ADVENTURES OF HELICOPTER JIM!

Helicopter Jim needed to use all the strength that he had from January. He held January in his hands and was able to move this huge structure that was made out of this purple amethyst kind of gem. He was able to surround the vault with this. He surrounded the vault with this structure, but now he needed to use it to crush the vault hoping that he would be able to bring all of the molecules together from July.

That was his hope, that was his thinking, and so he needed to, with all of his strength, with January helping him, use this structure. Helicopter Jim swam to one side of the structure, grabbed a hold of what looked like a huge beam... like a handle. He had to push it, and push it, and push it, and as he kept pushing it, he needed all the strength that he had. He pushed it, and he could see the structure slowly, slowly crushing the vault. He kept pushing with all of his might. He pushed, and pushed, and pushed, and as he pushed more, and more, he felt strength leaving him because it was so difficult, and he was getting tired.

He was now being drained of all of his strength, but he kept pushing it and pushing it. As he did so, he could hear something happening in the vault. He continued to crush the vault. As big as the vault was, he was able to crush the entire vault to a size way smaller than himself. After he did that, he released the handle from the structure. Then the structure was able to separate itself from the handle. Now, Helicopter Jim had to find a way to open the structure because within that structure, it possibly now held... the Stone of July. Helicopter Jim had to find a way to get to the Stone of July.

He couldn't pull open the structure because he didn't know where there would be an opening.

HJ: "Maybe I'm able to break through the structure."

He tried, and tried, and tried, and nothing happened, it was too strong for him. Then he remembered August, that it might be possible for him to retrieve July with August. He put January in his pouch and took out August, and he turned invisible. He reached through the structure, the amethyst structure, and he could feel around but nothing. He walked into the structure.

As he walked into the structure, he was able to locate where the Stone of July was, or what he thought was the Stone... because as he got closer, he noticed that it didn't look like the Stone of July, it looked different. In fact, when he got closer to it, he noticed that it wasn't like the other Stones that he had. What he saw was something encased in an amethyst box. He took a hold of it and he was able to retrieve the box and bring that out of the structure. Now, he had within his possession, something that was square. It wasn't like the other Stones, and he wondered...

HJ: "Why is it like this?"

Helicopter Jim put August back in his pouch and took out January. He had to figure a way to break this box hoping that July would be in the middle of this box. He didn't want to crush it so much that he might destroy the Stone of July. Helicopter Jim thought to himself, what could he possibly do? He had an idea. Helicopter Jim knew that the most powerful substance, is water. Helicopter Jim used the arm, once again, the beam, the handle, and pushed it in the other direction, opening up the structure. He pushed it and pushed it so much that he lost all strength. Even though he had January, he was losing strength. For some reason, his strength was being drained a lot quicker than normal, but he was able to get the structure open. What he did is he put the box in the structure as well as made sure that there was water all around the box...which wasn't that difficult because they were under water.

Helicopter Jim took out pieces from the structure so that when the structure would close around the box, there would still be water surrounding the box. If the structure could crush the water, and water being the most powerful substance, it would crush the box, and the box would break first before the structure would break.

Helicopter Jim made enough room in the structure so that water could be in there to surround the box, and he started to close the structure around the box.

He continued to push the handle and push the handle and push it. He pushed it so much that now the structure surrounded the box with water in it. Now he had to figure out a way to crush the structure enough where it would crush the water around the box and break the box. What Helicopter Jim did was he took the top part of the structure and the handle, and he began to crush them together. As he did so, the entire structure started to cave in on itself, and it became smaller and smaller because he was crushing the entire structure together.

He crushed it so much that he was able to use the water, and the pressure that came from the water, to crush the box. He could feel the box pop and explode on the inside. (EXPLODING POP SOUND F/X)

Helicopter Jim once again pushed the handle open so that the structure would open. He pushed it and pushed it and pushed it, and the structure opened up. As he did so, this bright purple glow, which was brighter than the entire place, was blinding him. As he was able to squint and look towards the light, he could see something that was in the middle of the structure.

As he got closer to it, he noticed that it was definitely...the Stone of July. He reached out and grabbed the Stone, and looked at it. It looked exactly like the other Stones. Helicopter Jim now held in his possession, the Stone of July!

AND THAT WILL BE THE NEXT ADVENTURE OF HELICOPTER JIM.

Adventure 108

On the last adventure of Helicopter Jim, Jim needed to find a way to retrieve the Stone of July. He used the structure to crush the vault, which he hoped would crush all of the molecules together.

Jim used January for increased strength and needed to make sure he crushed the box first, so that the Stone would be released.

He crushed it so much that he was able to use the water, and the pressure that came from the water, to crush the box. He could feel the box pop and explode on the inside. (EXPLODING POP SOUND F/X)

Helicopter Jim once again pushed the handle open so that the structure would open. He pushed it and pushed it and pushed it, and the structure opened up. As he did so, this bright purple glow, which was brighter than the entire place, was blinding him. As he was able to squint and look towards the light, he could see something that was in the middle of the structure.

As he got closer to it, he noticed that it was definitely...the Stone of July. He reached out and grabbed the Stone, and looked at it. It looked exactly like the other Stones. Helicopter Jim now held in his possession, the Stone of July!

AND NOW WE BEGIN THE ADVENTURES OF HELICOPTER JIM!

Then, all of a sudden, the walls began to shake and everything around Jim became so bright. Then, the walls began to tremble and then the walls fell down. (BRGSHHHH!) Jim didn't know what was going on. He didn't understand what was happening. He was afraid that something was going to happen to the palace. When he turned around, he could see everyone looking at him.

HJ: "What just happened?"

QUEEN AVEHI: "Well, basically what you did is make sure that the Stone could never again have the chance to be stuck in the vault or possibly destroyed somehow. Only the Chosen One was able to close the vault."

PRINCESS EVA: "Are you okay, Jim? Is everything okay?"

HJ: "Yeah... everything is fine. I feel fine. In fact, I don't know, for some reason, I feel like it's, it's doing something to me. I don't know. I feel stronger. I feel energized. I don't know. I don't know what it is."

SCOTT: "Well, you look different too. You actually look stronger. I don't know what it is, but you just look a little different."

MR. CAPE: "It could possibly be that with every Stone that Jim is retrieving, because he's the Chosen One, it also is becoming a part of who he is."

QUEEN AVEHI: "Well, after all these years, finally, the Stone of July is in the possession of the Chosen One. Come, we must celebrate with the people!"

The Queen, Princess Eva, Helicopter Jim, Scott, Mikhail, and Mr. Cape, along with Advan and Targy, follow the Queen and head out.

They all swam to a large area where people could gather. It was amazing. Even though they were underwater, there were still underwater lakes, creatures that they had never seen before. As they gathered together, the Queen stood high above the people on a beautiful structure made of dark purple amethyst crystals and made the announcement to the people.

QUEEN AVEHI: "People of Amethyst City, we have now been able to fulfill our responsibility of being the guardians of the Stone of July."

Many of the people didn't understand what she was talking about because they didn't know what was going on. They just knew that earlier the Queen's sister came and was up to no good. She was doing something evil and the people were afraid. They didn't know what to think.

Now, because of the Queen mentioning to them that the Chosen One now has the Stone, they started to realize that something good was happening. Then some of the people shouted, "What are you talking about? Are you saying that the Chosen One is here?" Others started to talk, "There is no Chosen One. After all these years, where would the Chosen One come from?" People were having mixed feelings and mixed emotions and perspectives because there were some people who doubted that the Chosen One even existed.

The Queen quieted the people…

QUEEN AVEHI: "Today, the prophecy has been fulfilled. These people next to me are our friends. They come from a far place."

Then she motioned to Helicopter Jim to come forward. He came forward to where the Queen was standing…

QUEEN AVEHI: "Ladies and gentlemen, this is the Chosen

One. He has retrieved the Stone of July from the vault."

Jim started waving to the people...

HJ: "Hey, everybody. Yes. I got the Stone. Here it is."

He held up the Stone of July and the people were in awe. They were wondering, "How could this be?" They weren't even prepared for it.

As Jim held up the Stone, it began to shine brightly, a bright purple. Then, and only then did the people truly realize that the Stone of July had been retrieved by the Chosen One. Now they started to cheer and everyone is cheering and shouting, and dancing, and singing because of the prophecy being fulfilled.

QUEEN AVEHI: "Although we celebrate, we still know that my sister and Dayor will not give up, trying to retrieve the Stone of July. You need to be careful Jim and be on the lookout for them, but for now, you need to... quickly... go and look for the other Stones. But before you leave, I have something to show you."

She took Helicopter Jim and everyone else to another place in her Palace. As they exited the area where they were, they had to swim down this long, deep corridor. As they're swimming down, they notice how incredibly beautiful the place is. Everywhere was glowing with purple, amethyst crystals, everywhere. As they're swimming down, they're going so far down...

HJ: "Where are we going?"

AND THAT WILL BE THE NEXT ADVENTURE OF HELICOPTER JIM.

Adventure 109

On the last adventure of Helicopter Jim, Jim was able to retrieve the Stone of July. Queen Avehi brings Jim to the people so they can celebrate.

The Queen turns to Helicopter Jim...

QUEEN AVEHI: "Although we celebrate, we still know that my sister and Dayor will not give up, trying to retrieve the Stone of July. You need to be careful Jim and be on the lookout for them, but for now, you need to... quickly... go and look for the other Stones. But before you leave, I have something to show you."

She took Helicopter Jim and everyone else to another place in her Palace. As they exited the area where they were, they had to swim down this long, deep corridor. As they're swimming down, they notice how incredibly beautiful the place is. Everywhere was glowing with purple, amethyst crystals, everywhere. As they're swimming down, they're going so far down...

HJ: "Where are we going?"

AND NOW WE BEGIN THE ADVENTURES OF HELICOPTER JIM!

As they go deeper and deeper, they come into this place where it is massive and huge, and a big opening. At the bottom, they see an area that has 12 Pillars. They swim all the way down to the bottom.

QUEEN AVEHI: "These are the 12 Pillars of the Stones of

the Months."

MIKHAIL: "What are the 12 Pillars for? I have never heard of the 12 Pillars."

QUEEN AVEHI: "There are only certain things that were given to us, as well as to all the different kings and protectors. This way each protector or king would make sure that they took care of their responsibility rather than worrying about everyone else's."

MR. CAPE: "What are the 12 Pillars for?"

QUEEN AVEHI: "The 12 Pillars are to understand the value behind the Stones and who the protectors are. Each Pillar will help Jim to know who he can trust as well as where he needs to go."

PRINCESS EVA: "You know where all the other Stones are?"

QUEEN AVEHI: "No, I don't. The Pillars don't tell me where the Stones are. The Pillars will only tell the Chosen One where the Stones are."

HJ: "What do I do?"

QUEEN AVEHI: "I'm not sure...but we need to leave this area and leave you alone with the Pillars. Then you're just going to have to figure it out."

HJ: "That's fine with me. I'd gone this far without knowing what to do, so I guess I'll just trust what you're saying."

Everyone swam back up and left the area where Helicopter Jim was. Jim, once again, finds himself alone. But this time, he's with the 12 Pillars.

HJ: (TALKING TO HIMSELF) "Okay, I'm with the 12 Pillars, where do I begin?"

He walks to one of the Pillars and stands in front of it...but nothing happens. He touches it and nothing happens.

HJ: (TALKING TO HIMSELF) "Why doesn't anything happen? Well, maybe I'll use the Stone of July, but the Stone of July... doesn't it increase- give strength to others? Something like that? Why would I need- well, I'll just try it. I'll just try it."

He takes out July. The moment he takes out July from his pouch, everything around him and all that is glowing around him, and all of the amethyst crystals... dim, but not so much that it's now dark. It just dims to where he can see just enough. Helicopter Jim holds July in his hands. And then, all of a sudden...

AND THAT WILL BE THE NEXT ADVENTURE OF HELICOPTER JIM.

Adventure 110

On the last adventure of Helicopter Jim, Queen Avehi gave Jim one more thing. She took him down this long corridor into this other area deep under the Palace where there were beautiful glowing purple, amethyst crystals, everywhere. As they're swimming down, they're going so far down and eventually come to the bottom where there are 12 Pillars.

Jim has to figure out what to do. He takes out July. And the moment he takes out July from his pouch, everything around him and all that is glowing around him, and all of the amethyst crystals... dim, but not so much that it's now dark. It just dims to where he can see just enough. Helicopter Jim holds July in his hands. And then, all of a sudden...

AND NOW WE BEGIN THE ADVENTURES OF HELICOPTER JIM!

And then, all of a sudden...out of the Stone comes this amazing stream of light and it shoots out of the Stone, and starts to inscribe on the Pillars. It etches into the Pillars, some form of writing.

From the Stone, these streams of light etched every single Pillar. Helicopter Jim is holding the Stone and all of the Pillars are being etched from the Stone, and light is shooting from the Stone. Helicopter Jim can't even look because it's so bright. He also feels energy drained from him.

As the Stone is etching into the Pillars, he collapses. He's lying on the ground, he has no more strength left.

Finally, the writing on the Pillars are done. Helicopter Jim has barely enough strength, so he puts July back into his pouch and grabs January. The moment he takes a hold of January, his strength increases...100%. (SOUND F/X OF STRENGTH RETURNING) He is now once again strong and vibrant, and full of energy and he can think clearer. He puts January back in his pouch, walks over to one of the Pillars and reads the Pillar.

The first Pillar he reads is the Stone of October. On the Pillar, it has the name and location of the Stone of October and the name of the king or the protector of the Stone. He goes to the next Pillar and he reads it. He goes to all of the Pillars and he reads the names of the ones protecting the Stone as well as the location and which world each Stone is on. He's trying to read the Pillars as fast as he can...but then he remembers...

HJ: "December! Where's December! (AS IF LOOKING FRANTICALLY) No, no, no, no, no...where's December?"

All of a sudden, all of the Pillars begin to shake and start to light up, and each Pillar lights up with the color of the Stone that it represents.

The Pillar of January glows a dark red. February bright turquoise. March, an unbelievable green. April, a golden-yellow. May, blue-green, which when blended with the water, looked amazing! June is an incredible blue. July shoots off such a powerful punch of purple. August, brightens up the entire place with a blinding white. September is a vibrant yellow. October releases fiery orange. November sends off a pretty pink glow. And December...a radiant bright red. And all the Pillars light up. Then, each Pillar becomes very bright, and begins to disintegrate...

HJ: "No, no, no....wait...December!"

The Pillars turn into this fine sand. But because it's underwater, it looks milky in the water. Then, it gets sucked into the Stone of July that Helicopter Jim is holding. He looks at the Stone of July, and he can see that the 12 Pillars, which are so small now, are swirling in the Stone.

Each of the Pillars are now in his possession. Helicopter Jim then exits where he is and swims up all the way back to where the Queen and everyone else is.

PRINCESS EVA: "What happened? What did you do?"

HJ: "You wouldn't believe what just happened. There were these 12 Pillars that popped up and each one of the Pillars was inscribed by this light that shot out of the Stone of July and it etched into each Pillar, the name of the protectors of each Stone as well as the location of each Stone."

SCOTT: "All of the Stones?"

HJ: "Yes."

SCOTT: "Even December? Because that's the one that is the confusing one."

MR. CAPE: "Yes, what about December?"

HJ: "I couldn't get to December in time...but if you look at it in the Stone of July, that's the only one that has nothing etched on it. I don't know why, I don't know why it's blank. I was trying to get to December...but why isn't December etched? It's in the Stone, you can see it, it's in the Stone of July."

MIKHAIL: "Well, let's not worry about that right now. The

main thing is you're okay and you have the 12 Pillars. That is amazing."

HJ: "Amazing and strange."

MR. CAPE: "What do you mean?"

HJ: "Well...amazing that I have the 12 Pillars, strange that June was the only one that read something weird."

SCOTT: "Like what? What do you mean weird?"

HJ: "It said, 'Life is in the eye.' Whatever that means."

Helicopter Jim thanked Queen Avehi…

QUEEN AVEHI: "No, Jim, thank you...and good luck on your journey. We are all supporting you."

Helicopter Jim, Mr. Cape, Princess Eva, Scott, and Mikhail went through Amethyst City to head back to (HELICOPTER NAME). The people of Amethyst City came out and began to cheer them on. Helicopter Jim and the rest of the team swam all the way back to (HELICOPTER NAME) and climbed in...

HJ: "You wouldn't believe what we just went through and what just happened...It was amazing!"

HELICOPTER: "Well, I'm glad you're okay."

HJ: "I have in my possession… (USE A DRAMATIC VOICE) located in the Stone of July...The 12 Pillars...which represent those who protect the Stones or the kings, I guess, who watch over the Stones."

HELICOPTER: "Well done with retrieving July! As far as the 12 Pillars...what you have in your possession is called the 12

Protective Pillars."

SCOTT: "That sounds pretty cool. What are the 12 Protective Pillars?"

AND THAT WILL BE THE NEXT ADVENTURE OF HELICOPTER JIM.

Adventure 111

On the last adventure of Helicopter Jim, Jim was able to collect the 12 Pillars, which turned into fine sand, and was now inside of the Stone of July.

Jim made his way back up to where Queen Avehi, Mr. Cape, Princess Eva, Scott, and Mikhail were. And they all said goodbye to the Queen of Amethyst City.

Helicopter Jim, Mr. Cape, Princess Eva, Scott, and Mikhail went through Amethyst City to head back to (HELICOPTER NAME). The people of Amethyst City came out and began to cheer them on. Helicopter Jim and the rest of the team swam all the way back to (HELICOPTER NAME) and climbed in...

HJ: "You wouldn't believe what we just went through and what just happened...It was amazing!"

HELICOPTER: "Well, I'm glad you're okay."

HJ: "I have in my possession... (USE A DRAMATIC VOICE) located in the Stone of July...The 12 Pillars...which represent those who protect the Stones or the kings, I guess, who watch over the Stones."

HELICOPTER: "Well done with retrieving July! As far as the 12 Pillars...what you have in your possession is called the 12 Protective Pillars."

SCOTT: "That sounds pretty cool. What are the 12 Protective pillars?"

AND NOW WE BEGIN THE ADVENTURES OF HELICOPTER JIM!

HELICOPTER: "Well Scott, the Protective Pillars were created to assist the Chosen One as well as to give special power to each protector for being faithful and diligent to protect each Stone. Once Jim restores all the Stones, then all the Pillars will go back to the protectors and that Pillar, each Pillar will be a reminder of the peace and restoration that was brought to the entire universe. Because everyone worked together to support the Chosen One, every time people see the Pillar, they will remember that peace and unity prevailed."

So as the team left Amethyst City, they needed to figure out where to go next. Princess Eva had an idea…

PRINCESS EVA: "Jim, if we are to retrieve the rest of the Stones, we need to figure out a way to…to utilize all that we have in our favor. What I mean is, we need to get more organized. We're not…we're not really organized."

SCOTT: (SOUNDING IRRITATED) "Organized! What do you mean organized? Do you… do you realize what just happened with not just retrieving the Stone of July, but ever since day one, there has been *no* organization, what do you mean *get* organized? Jim *found* himself on this journey, he didn't *choose* it!"

MR. CAPE: "I think what she means Scott, is that with all that we have, we can utilize what we have to our advantage. Just think of what we do have, what…what…what we have that can be used, because she's right, where *do* we go next?"

MIKHAIL: "Well, if we have in our possession…if Jim has in his possession, January, February, March, August, and now July, he now possesses five of the Stones… that's not that bad. He already... he already has them so why don't we- why don't we work with what we know of? We know where May is and how to retrieve May, let's go back to the Rock of Rhone and get May."

So that was their plan, they needed to head back to the Rock of Rhone. So (HELICOPTER NAME) set course to go back to the cave where they would be able to go back to the Rock of Rhone. They needed to wait for the right time so that the Jump Cave would be able to take them to the Rock of Rhone.

So as they're heading toward the cave, (HELICOPTER NAME) senses something on the Trxsol and a light starts flashing and beeping (MAKE BEEPING SOUND F/X).

HJ: "What-what is that beeping? I've never heard that beeping before!"

HELICOPTER: "That's a warning that there is something coming towards us."

SCOTT: "What do you mean 'something coming towards us?' What is... what is... what-what-what could be coming towards us?"

HELICOPTER: "It seems like there is a massive…

AND THAT WILL BE THE NEXT ADVENTURE OF HELICOPTER JIM.

Adventure 112

On the last adventure of Helicopter Jim, Jim was able to understand more about the 12 Protective Pillars and what exactly they were for.

They made the decision to go back to the Rock of Rhone to retrieve the Stone of May. So they needed to go through the Jump Cave to get there.

So as they're heading toward the cave, (HELICOPTER NAME) senses something on the Trxsol and a light starts flashing and beeping (MAKE BEEPING SOUND F/X).

HJ: "What-what is that beeping? I've never heard that beeping before!"

HELICOPTER: "That's a warning that there is something coming towards us."

SCOTT: "What do you mean 'something coming towards us?' What is... what is... what-what-what could be coming towards us?"

HELICOPTER: "It seems like there is a massive...

AND NOW WE BEGIN THE ADVENTURES OF HELICOPTER JIM!

HELICOPTER: "It seems like there is a massive...flock of birds coming our way."

SCOTT: "Birds!? Okay, well, no big deal, I mean, we're in... we're safe in here. Why...why...why is that a concern?"

HELICOPTER: "It wouldn't be so bad if it was one or two,

but there are thousands of them coming our way."

SCOTT: "Okay, but do you know why they're coming? Or...or...or if we're in danger?"

HELICOPTER: "That's the problem. I detect that they're coming for *us*."

SCOTT: "Wait a minute, wait a minute, what do you mean they're coming for *us*? Why would they be coming for *us*?"

HELICOPTER: "Because Jim just retrieved the Stone of July and I'm pretty sure Dayor knows what's happening. I'm pretty sure the Queen's sister may have said something. So brace yourselves because this is going to be a rough ride."

PRINCESS EVA: (WITH A STERN VOICE) "Okay, guys, buckle up, this is going to be a tough one!"

HELICOPTER: "There are thousands of them. Here, let me pull it up on the screen."

So (HELICOPTER NAME) pulls it up on the screen and everyone can see what is happening and as they look at the screen, they see thousands of these birds coming their way and these are weird looking...they have large claws, large beaks, and their eyes are so small, but they have multiple eyes and they just look weird...

HJ: "What kind of birds are those? And why are they so-- they're dark, but as they flap their wings there's like little sparks or... What is that? Like lights coming from them? What... what is that?"

MIKHAIL: "These birds are electrical birds. They're able to send little shocks of electricity, that's why we're in danger and they're heading our way pretty fast. I can sense that they want to harm us."

MR. CAPE: "Well, we need to get ready then because if...if something happens to (HELICOPTER NAME) and you know, we're not able to...to...to function, then we're going to have to... we're going to have to do something."

And so, as they're flying, Helicopter Jim has a thought...

HJ: "Hey, what if...I mean, would-would it... would it work if... if we were to use August? Because if...if we use August, maybe we'll all turn invisible, can...can we try that?"

HELICOPTER: "It's worth a try, let's see what happens...and you better hurry up because here they come!"

So Helicopter Jim takes out August and everyone grabs each other's hands and the moment that happens, they all disappear including (HELICOPTER NAME) and all of a sudden they feel a bump to the helicopter and (HELICOPTER NAME) starts to go faster and faster and for some reason, the birds can still sense that they're there.

So the birds start to attack (HELICOPTER NAME) and Jim is thinking...

HJ: "Why is this not working? How can they even see us?"

HELICOPTER: "Because they're not looking with their eyes. They are sensing our presence. Those aren't eyes on their heads. They're using sonar, so they can still detect us."

And the birds start to attack and they're shocking (HELICOPTER NAME) one after another. (BZZZ BZZZZ)

HELICOPTER: "This is not good for my system... that they're shocking me like this. We might lose a little bit of control, so Jim, you're going to have to navigate and fly very well. You're going to have to take over so that we can get to where we need to go."

So Helicopter Jim thinks very carefully about what he needs to do because he has to fly by thought. And so Helicopter Jim thought...

HJ: "Wait a minute, what if we were to do this? Instead of us trying to run from them, why don't we lead them somewhere? Because if they're flying by sonar and if they're following us through sonar, let's lead them somewhere."

SCOTT: "Where are we going to lead them? Where...where...where...where are we gonna go?"

HJ: "I have an idea, let's fly very high, and let's see how high they can go."

SCOTT: "You're gonna do what!?"

And so Helicopter Jim takes them all to a higher elevation and he continues to go up higher and higher. As he's doing so, all of the birds continue to follow them higher and higher.

PRINCESS EVA: "It's not working, what are you trying to do?"

HJ: "Watch this."

All of a sudden Helicopter Jim turns them around from going higher and takes a nose dive straight down towards the water. And as he does so, all of the birds follow him and they go faster and faster.

SCOTT: "Jim, what are you doing? You're gonna crash right..right into the water...you can't pull up at this speed and make the turn!"

HJ: "(HELICOPTER NAME) get ready…"

HELICOPTER: "Get ready for what?"

AND THAT WILL BE THE NEXT ADVENTURE OF HELICOPTER JIM.

Adventure 113

On the last adventure of Helicopter Jim, (HELICOPTER NAME) detected something on the Trxsol as they were heading to the Jump Cave to go back to the Rock of Rhone.

(HELICOPTER NAME) detected that it was a massive flock of birds. Not just any flock of birds, these were electrical birds.

They began to attack (HELICOPTER NAME), even though Jim tried using August to disappear...the birds could still sense where they were because they use sonar rather than eyesight.

HJ: "I have an idea, let's fly very high, and let's see how high they can go."

SCOTT: "You're gonna do what!?"

And so Helicopter Jim takes them all to a higher elevation and he continues to go up higher and higher. As he's doing so, all of the birds continue to follow them higher and higher.

PRINCESS EVA: "It's not working, what are you trying to do?"

HJ: "Watch this."

All of a sudden Helicopter Jim turns them around from going higher and takes a nose dive straight down towards the water. And as he does so, all of the birds follow him and they go faster and faster.

SCOTT: "Jim, what are you doing? You're gonna crash right..right into the water...you can't pull up at this speed and make the turn!"

HJ: "(HELICOPTER NAME) get ready…"

HELICOPTER: "Get ready for what?"

AND NOW WE BEGIN THE ADVENTURES OF HELICOPTER JIM!

HJ: "We're not gonna crash into the water, we're gonna dive straight into the water."

SCOTT: "What do you mean right into the water? You're gonna go back under the water?"

HJ: "Yup. If they're following us at this speed with sonar, we're gonna lead them right into the water. (HELICOPTER NAME) steady, steady…(DESCENDING RAPIDLY SOUND F/X) Now! Speed-Jet Submarine!"

(HELICOPTER CHANGING SOUND F/X)

(HELICOPTER NAME) changes into a Speed-Jet Submarine...

Helicopter Jim takes (HELICOPTER NAME) and plunges right into the water. (SPLASH SOUND) And sure enough, all of the birds follow him and go under the water.

But because they are electric birds, they all electrocute one another and they're all stunned. Helicopter Jim shoots back out of the water (EXIT WATER SOUND F/X) and changes back to a helicopter (HELICOPTER CHANGING SOUND F/X) all of the birds are now floating on the water and they cannot fly because they are all stunned.

SCOTT: "Woohoo! Good job, Jim. Brilliant idea!"

MR. CAPE: "That was uh...that was a good… a good idea!"

MIKHAIL: (LAUGHING WITH JOY) "Jim, that was genius...super intelligent!"

PRINCESS EVA: "Now that's what I call flying! Impressive!"

HELICOPTER: "Okay, we need to get to the cave because the portal for us to get to the Rock of Rhone is going to close soon."

So they head to the cave and sure enough, they made it by a couple of minutes.

They enter the cave and they are transported to the Rock of Rhone once again. And so, as they get to the Rock of Rhone, they head out of the cave and head towards the area where the Stone of May is, and they go into the large cave and they can only go so far with (HELICOPTER NAME).

And so they all exit (HELICOPTER NAME) and sure enough, right before them is the tribal leader. And the tribal leader greets them, nods his head, and smiles. He is glad to see them again.

HJ: "It's so good to see you again!"

And the tribal leader nods his head...

HJ: "Can you take us to the Stone of May?"

And the tribal leader nods his head, "Yes."

And so as they're heading towards May, (HELICOPTER NAME) stays in the large cavern area where all of the drawings are.

And so they follow the tribal leader and they go through this big area and through the big doors that lead into the area where the Stone of May is. So Helicopter Jim follows, and they come to the Stone of May, which is encased in the crystallized rock formation. And Helicopter Jim looks at the tribal leader and asks...

HJ: "Would you give me the honor and permission to retrieve the Stone of May?"

The tribal leader smiles, takes off the amulet around his neck and places it on the rock formation, and all of a sudden, the rock formation begins to tremble and shake. And as it's shaking, the rock formation begins to- it looks like it's melting, but really what's happening is it's starting to crumble. And as it's doing that, the rock formation turns into fine dust-like particles of crystals. And the Stone of May is exposed.

The tribal leader looks at Jim and motions to him to retrieve the Stone of May. Helicopter Jim reaches out his hand, puts it on the Stone of May and the moment he does that, all of a sudden this huge sound wave reverberates from the Stone of May [REVERBERATING SOUND] and it hits all of them, including the tribal leader and the entire tribe...all those who were surrounding them.

Helicopter Jim is wondering what just happened? He is now holding the Stone of May.

SCOTT: "What was that!"

HJ: "I'm not sure...something happened though."

MR. CAPE: "Are you okay?"

SCOTT: "Yeah...almost pee pee my pants, but I'll recover..."

PRINCESS EVA: "Not you Scott...Jim, are you okay!"

HJ: "Yeah...I'm okay."

Jim turns to the tribal leader…

HJ: "Thank you so much. Thank you. Thank you. Thank you."

The tribal leader looks confused and holds his throat.

HJ: "Are you-are you okay? Is everything okay?"

AND THAT WILL BE THE NEXT ADVENTURE OF HELICOPTER JIM.

Adventure 114

On the last adventure of Helicopter Jim, Jim was able to ask the tribal leader for the Stone of May, and the tribal leader gave him permission to retrieve May.

As Helicopter Jim took ahold of the Stone, and as he does, a huge sound wave reverberates from the Stone and sends a sound wave that hits everyone.

Helicopter Jim is wondering what just happened? He is now holding the Stone of May.

SCOTT: "What was that!"

HJ: "I'm not sure...something happened though."

MR. CAPE: "Are you okay?"

SCOTT: "Yeah...almost pee pee my pants, but I'll recover..."

PRINCESS EVA: "Not you Scott...Jim, are you okay!"

HJ: "Yeah...I'm okay."

Jim turns to the tribal leader...

HJ: "Thank you so much. Thank you. Thank you. Thank you."

The tribal leader looks confused and holds his throat.

HJ: "Are you-are you okay? Is everything okay?"

AND NOW WE BEGIN THE ADVENTURES OF HELICOPTER JIM!

And the tribal leader kept holding his throat and he's feeling his throat. And he starts to clear his throat. (CLEAR YOUR

THROUGH)

And Scott looks at the tribal leader too...

SCOTT: "What's-what's wrong with your throat? You're freaking me out a little."

And the tribal leader looks at Helicopter Jim and speaks...

TRIBAL LEADER: (STRENUOUSLY SPEAKING) "Something just happened in my throat when you retrieved the Stone of May... and now I am able to speak."

HJ: "Yeah, what-what-what just happened? Why, you can speak now! What is- what is that all about? So that's a- that's a good thing...right?"

The tribal leader turns around and sees all of his men and all of them are touching their throat because they can feel something too. And all of a sudden, all of the men are able to speak too. The tribal leader looks at Helicopter Jim and nods his head and speaks again...

TRIBAL LEADER: (STILL STRAINING A LITTLE) "I don't know what happened or how this came about, but this changes everything about us as a people. And we are grateful for every single one of you. Jim, you definitely are... the Chosen One."

Not only is Jim grateful, he is also aware that he still needs to find the other Stones. The tribal leader brings Helicopter Jim to the cave where all of the drawings are...

TRIBAL LEADER: "The Stone of December is the one Stone everyone is curious about. One thing we know Jim, if you look at all of these drawings, it all has to do with what is necessary for the Chosen One to be able to retrieve the Stones. Don't forget who you are and that there are so many people supporting you, believing in you. Countless amounts of thought and energy went toward looking forward to helping the Chosen One retrieve the Stones. Although we're all counting on you, you're the only one who will be able to bring clarity to what the Stone of December is all about. I've studied these drawings all my life. One thing I know for sure, is that everything rests on the Stone of December....everything rests on December. We know you will do well."

With that, Helicopter Jim left the cave, got into (HELICOPTER NAME) and they took off.

HELICOPTER: "So, Jim, where to now? Where do we go?"

HJ: "We need to go to the caves. We need to go to the Jump Caves. We have to find the next Stone. As I looked at the drawings in the cave, there was one drawing that caught my attention. I think that's what the tribal leader was trying to tell me. He was showing me that these drawings were not just drawings to have, or drawings to keep a record of history, but it was also a way for me to maximize my strengths, to mature, to gain wisdom, as well as to utilize you to your fullest potential. I don't even know how to maximize all of your different abilities."

PRINCESS EVA: "There are some things that we should be able to do with (HELICOPTER NAME)...because we're more familiar now with the various functions you have... but, you're more aware than us Jim. It's just knowing what to do and how to accomplish it. When I looked at the different drawings of what you're able to do (HELICOPTER NAME), we haven't even begun to utilize all that you're capable of doing."

MR. CAPE: "That is true. It could possibly be because we really didn't need to."

SCOTT: "Well, speak for yourself. I think we could have done a lot more. If what those drawings and markings on those cave walls showed us is true, then there's pretty much nothing (HELICOPTER NAME) cannot do, but at the same time, I don't want to be in any situation where we're going to have to use all the abilities of this helicopter. No offense, (HELICOPTER NAME), I'm just saying that I would love to *not* be in situations where we would need to use or maximize your fullest potential. For instance, that drawing of spinning...yeah, not up for throwing up. Although I would love to see it, I think I'm okay without having to use all of your abilities."

Helicopter Jim made his way toward the Jump Cave. He needed to find the other Stones and with the 12 Pillars, he was able to know, at least, what world they would need to go to.

AND THAT WILL BE THE NEXT ADVENTURE OF HELICOPTER JIM.

Adventure 115

On the last adventure of Helicopter Jim, the tribal leader gave Jim some advice about the Stone of December, while reminding Jim of who he is as the Chosen One.

Jim realized that the drawings in the cave wasn't just to keep record, it was also about helping Jim reach his fullest potential and to show some of the abilities that (HELICOPTER NAME) could do..

PRINCESS EVA: "There are some things that we should be able to do with (HELICOPTER NAME)...because we're more familiar now with the various functions you have... but, you're more aware than us Jim. It's just knowing what to do and how to accomplish it. When I looked at the different drawings of what you're able to do (HELICOPTER NAME), we haven't even begun to utilize all that you're capable of doing."

MR. CAPE: "That is true. It could possibly be because we really didn't need to."

SCOTT: "Well, speak for yourself. I think we could have done a lot more. If what those drawings and markings on those cave walls showed us is true, then there's pretty much nothing (HELICOPTER NAME) cannot do, but at the same time, I don't want to be in any situation where we're going to have to use all the abilities of this helicopter. No offense, (HELICOPTER NAME), I'm just saying that I would love to *not* be in situations where we would need to use or maximize your fullest potential. For instance, that drawing of spinning...yeah, not up for throwing up. Although I would love to see it, I think I'm okay without having to use all of your abilities."

Helicopter Jim made his way toward the Jump Cave. He needed to find the other Stones and with the 12 Pillars, he was able to know, at least, what world they would need to go to.

AND NOW WE BEGIN THE ADVENTURES OF HELICOPTER JIM!

HJ: "I say we go back to Diamond Crust. You haven't seen your father in a long time, Princess. Maybe it's a good time for us to go back and at least drop by and say hello. We know that the Stone of June is there, and the Stone of September. Where exactly? Who knows?"

PRINCESS EVA: "But at the same time, we're here in Waterworks, and the Stone of November is here. Why don't we just stay here and look for November?"

HJ: "That's fine with me. We can do that. Just being attacked by birds kind of freaked me out. We can do that. I just thought maybe we can get out of here for a little bit, and let things calm down because Dayor knows we're here and maybe we can come back later. That's just a thought. I'm not sure if everyone wants to do that."

MR. CAPE: "I'm fine with going back to Diamond Crust."

Everybody agreed.

SCOTT: "Yes, I agree too. Let's get out of here! I don't want to have those birds come back to get us. We can always come back here and look for the Stone of November. That'll be fine. Although, on the other hand, if we do find November, then it's going to help us with December, so we really need to think this through."

HJ: "That is true. I do understand that each Stone is going to do something to help us with the next Stone or at least help us along the way. How about we go to Diamond Crust and then go from there."

They all agreed.

So they head to the Jump Cave and (HELICOPTER NAME) enters the cave and waits for the perfect time and transitions to Diamond Crust. (MAKE A SOUND F/X OF TRANSITIONING) They go through the portal and now, they're on Diamond Crust.

PRINCESS EVA: "It is so good to be back home. I miss my home. I can't wait to see my father."

They fly towards where Princess Eva's family is, where the Emperor is, Diamond Falls.

They see one of the giant warriors near the waterfall and they're about to land nearby...

PRINCESS EVA: "Hey (HELICOPTER NAME), can I speak to my friend down there? He looks a little alarmed."

HELICOPTER: "Absolutely Princess...go ahead."

PRINCESS: (SPEAKING THROUGH THE OUTSIDE LOUDSPEAKER) "Zaiah! Zaiah it's me, Princess Eva! Wait, we're going to land near you...don't attack us!"

ZAIAH: "Princess! Is that really you?! I hope so, because I was about to beat this thing down!"

Helicopter Jim slowly lands and the Princess is the first one out and runs toward Zaiah...

PRINCESS EVA: "Zaiah! How are you doing?"

ZAIAH: "I'm doing fine princess. It is so good to see you."

He bows down and then picks her up and gives her a big hug.

ZAIAH: "It is so good to see you too Jim, as well as everyone else. I see you have some new friends."

MIKHAIL: "I'm Mikhail...Wow! I thought I was tall!"

ZAIAH: "It's good to meet you...What brings you guys back to Diamond Falls?"

HJ: "Well, we realized that even though we have the Stone of February, there are two more Stones here on Diamond Crust."

ZAIAH: "Really? That's incredible. Come, we must see your father, Princess. And where's Big Chief?"

PRINCESS EVA: "He decided that his people needed him, so when Jim retrieved the Stone of March, and restored the land of Rhone, Big Chief felt he needed to stay with them."

ZAIAH: "I understand...I'm sure Big Chief made the right decision. So, you got the Stone of March Jim? Well done!"

Zaiah takes them to his boat so he can take them to the entrance of Diamond Falls.

HJ: "Hey Zaiah, now that I have the Stone of February, we can all walk on water with you...we don't need your boat."

ZAIAH: "That's true! (SARCASTICALLY) But then again, who's going to have to walk all the way back here to guard the entrance? (POINT TO YOURSELF) This guy.'"

HJ: (POINT AND TAKE A BREATH) "Riiiiiiight. Okay, we'll get in. Come on everyone...get in."

SCOTT: "Whoa, whoa, whoa...no, you guys can get into the boat...Jim and I are going to walk on the water."

HJ: "Really Scott!?"

SCOTT: "Hey, ever since I was a kid, I always wanted to walk on water...

PRINCESS EVA: "Scott, you are a kid."

SCOTT: (SARCASTIC LAUGH) "Ha ha ha...so funny this Princess...besides, other than Zaiah and the other giant warrior, no one has ever walked on water before."

HJ: "Well...there was this one Man who did..."

SCOTT: "Awe c'mon Jim! Let's just do it...we're wasting time."

HJ: "Ok, but the Stones aren't so that we play around with it...we have it for a specific reason."

SCOTT: "And I'm alllllll for that buddy! And besides, we need to test it and practice just in case we need it in the future."

Helicopter Jim takes out the Stone of February and he and Scott begin to walk on water.

SCOTT: "Yeah buddy...that's what I'm talking about! Guys, you should try this!"

And they all walk on water...Zaiah joins them too.

SCOTT: "Hey Jim, watch this."

HJ: "Watch what?"

AND THAT WILL BE THE NEXT ADVENTURE OF HELICOPTER JIM.

Adventure 116

On the last adventure of Helicopter Jim, they decided to head back to Diamond Crust to search for June and September. As they go through the Portal, they find themselves in Princess Eva's homeland.

As they approach Diamond Falls, Princess Eva sees Zaiah and they land near him. They all greet Zaiah and are about to make their way to see the Emperor.

Jim wants to use February to walk on water, but Zaiah convinces Jim to use the boat so that he doesn't have to walk back by himself. Scott would rather walk on water...

SCOTT: "Hey, ever since I was a kid, I always wanted to walk on water...

PRINCESS EVA: "Scott, you are a kid."

SCOTT: (SARCASTIC LAUGH) "Ha ha ha...so funny this Princess...besides, other than Zaiah and the other giant warrior, no one has ever walked on water before."

HJ: "Well...there was this one Man who did..."

SCOTT: "Awe c'mon Jim! Let's just do it...we're wasting time."

HJ: "Ok, but the Stones aren't so that we play around with it...we have it for a specific reason."

SCOTT: "And I'm allllllll for that buddy! And besides, we need to test it and practice just in case we need it in the future."

Helicopter Jim takes out the Stone of February and he and

Scott begin to walk on water.

SCOTT: "Yeah buddy...that's what I'm talking about! Guys, you should try this!"

And they all walk on water...Zaiah joins them too.

SCOTT: "Hey Jim, watch this."

HJ: "Watch what?"

AND NOW WE BEGIN THE ADVENTURES OF HELICOPTER JIM!

Scott runs full speed and slides on the surface of the water…

SCOTT: "How's this! Woohoo!"

Just then, because Scott is too far from Jim, he falls right into the water and goes under...and now he has to swim back, closer to Jim to get back on the water.

Everyone is laughing…

SCOTT: (SHIVERING) "Yeah...very funny...it's cold you know!"

PRINCESS EVA: "Yeah...I know! I grew up here!"

SCOTT: (SHIVERING) "Well, at least I know how far I can go from you before I sink. Zaiah, come here...give me a hug...I need some heat."

ZAIAH: (HAND GESTURES AS IF TO GIVE A HUG) "Bring it in Scott."

Zaiah gives Scott a big hug...

They all enter the boat and head to the front of the waterfall. Zaiah stops and claps his hands once (CLAP HANDS) and the waterfall splits open.

HJ: "Wait...how come the last time, the other warrior clapped seven times?"

ZAIAH: "He was in training at the time...he's down to three now."

As they went through the opening of the waterfall, they enter this massive cave, including (HELICOPTER NAME), who's following behind closely. As they went through, the waterfall slowly closed behind them.

Everything around them is sparkling with what looks like diamonds. Everything is shining, even though there's no light coming in from outside.

MIKHAIL: "This is unbelievable!"

HJ: "Pretty cool huh?"

As they enter Diamond Falls, as they're going through the waterfall, Helicopter Jim thinks to himself...

HJ: "Wait a minute, let's do something with the capabilities of (HELICOPTER NAME)."

Helicopter Jim is trying to figure out something...

HJ: "Can you transform into some kind of a boat or something? Can you change into a ship or something? Some of the drawings looked like boats and ships."

HELICOPTER: "Absolutely. Let me come next to you guys...jump in."

(HELICOPTER NAME) opens the doors and Jim jumps in.

PRINCESS EVA: "Wait…"

SCOTT: "Me too...wait!"

Scott and Princess Eva jump in too. (HELICOPTER NAME) puts on the screens, different shapes and different forms of ships and different boats.

HJ: "Oh... my... goodness, you have so many different forms. This is amazing. Look at this. You can even change yourself into like-- It looks almost like a pirate ship. You can do that too? Or even this one, look at this Princess…you can turn into a battleship too! Are you kidding me? You could have been a battleship all this time at Waterworks! We could have done a much better job if you were a battleship with those birds."

HELICOPTER: "I could have, but I'm leaving it up to you. You're the one that's going to need to use wisdom. I'm just going to follow your lead. Sure. I can do other things, but I'm going to follow your lead."

SCOTT: "Let me get this straight. All this time, you could have transformed into these different shapes of boats and ships? Look at that, even an underwater vehicle. Look at these underwater ones. Oh my goodness. You know what? That's okay. At least we know more of your capabilities."

HJ: "Hey, let's change into this one!"

(HELICOPTER NAME) Changes into this amazing boat.

(SOUND F/X OF CHANGING INTO A BOAT)

SCOTT: "What! That was A M A Z I N G ! You can change while we're still in you?"

HELICOPTER: "Yes I can."

By then they got closer to the city and sure enough, there was the Emperor right on the shoreline, waiting for the Princess, his daughter.

Princess Eva yells from afar…

PRINCESS EVA: "Daddy!"

AND THAT WILL BE THE NEXT ADVENTURE OF HELICOPTER JIM.

Adventure 117

On the last adventure of Helicopter Jim, Jim, Scott, Princess Eva, Mikhail, Mr. Cape and Zaiah were on their way to see the Emperor when Scott wanted to walk on water.

They also learned that (HELICOPTER NAME) was able to change into different kinds of boats and ships.

SCOTT: "Let me get this straight. All this time, you could have transformed into these different shapes of boats and ships? Look at that, even an underwater vehicle. Look at these underwater ones. Oh my goodness. You know what? That's okay. At least we know more of your capabilities."

HJ: "Hey, let's change into this one!"

(HELICOPTER NAME) Changes into this amazing boat.

(SOUND F/X OF CHANGING INTO A BOAT)

SCOTT: "What! That was A M A Z I N G ! You can change while we're still in you?"

HELICOPTER: "Yes I can."

By then they got closer to the city and sure enough, there was the Emperor right on the shoreline, waiting for the Princess, his daughter.

Princess Eva yells from afar...

PRINCESS EVA: "Daddy!"

AND NOW WE BEGIN THE ADVENTURE OF HELICOPTER JIM!

They're heading closer to shore and Helicopter Jim watches

Zaiah bring their boat to shore and dock right in front of the Emperor. Princess Eva jumps off of (HELICOPTER NAME) onto the dock, onto the pier where the Emperor is, runs to her father and gives him a big hug.

EMPEROR: "I missed you Eva…"

PRINCESS EVA: "I missed you too dad."

The Emperor turns to Helicopter Jim…

EMPEROR: "Jim, it is so good to see you. It's been a while. It's good to see all of you."

HJ: "It's so good to see you too Emperor!"

MIKHAIL: "By the way Emperor, I'm Mikhail…what an honor to meet you."

EMPEROR: "Thank you for keeping watch over Jim, my daughter, and the others…you're always welcomed here. Where's Big Chief?"

SCOTT: (SHORT AND SWEET TALK) "Not here…back on Rhone…long story. But he's doing good."

EMPEROR: "So what do I owe your visit? Why the surprise?"

HJ: "We've been all over the place. We retrieved a couple more Stones that had been around various places…(EXCITED) Oh, oh, oh, wait, wait, I was also able to retrieve… what is called… (SPEAKING DRAMATICALLY) the 12 Pillars!"

EMPEROR: "You retrieved the 12 Pillars! That is amazing! That is good news. And once all of the Stones are restored, the 12 Pillars are given to the protectors of the Stones."

HJ: "Yes, I know that. I found that out. It's a way to remind everyone of the peace and restoration that was brought to the entire universe."

EMPEROR: "True. That is true, but there's so much more to it than that."

HJ: "What do you mean there's so much more? That's pretty much all the information that I was given."

EMPEROR: "Right, because that's the information that you needed, but what you don't know is that once the 12 Pillars are given to the protectors, wherever those Pillars are, protects that area."

HJ: "Protects the area from what? Once the Stones are returned, you don't have to worry because then peace and unity will return, right? To the entire universe... so, what's the big deal?"

EMPEROR: "Yes, peace and unity will return to our universe."

HJ: "What do you mean... *our* universe? I don't get it. A universe is a universe. It's just one, so you should be safe, right? Who's going to attack you, Dayor? Once we return all the Stones, shouldn't everywhere be united and peaceful?"

EMPEROR: "Yes. In this universe, yes. However, there are multiverses."

SCOTT: "Wait a minute, wait a minute. Now I'm totally confused. The Rock of Rhone, Diamond Crust, Waterworks, aaaaand (SNAP FINGERS AS IF YOU'RE THINKING HARD) what was the other one? The volcano one, Magmatia, all of these four different worlds are not within one universe?"

EMPEROR: "No, no, no... they're all a part of the same universe. We're just not sure how many more universes there are... but we know for sure that the four worlds are all in the same universe...and most likely your world too."

Mr. Cape agreed with them.

AND THAT WILL BE THE NEXT ADVENTURE OF HELICOPTER JIM!

Adventure 118

On the last adventure of Helicopter Jim, Princess Eva was able to see her father, the Emperor, as well as the rest of the team. Jim learned a little more about the 12 Protective Pillars, and that wherever they are, it protects that area.

The Emperor also explained to Jim that there are multiverses...which caused Scott to ask some good questions...

SCOTT: "Wait a minute, wait a minute. Now I'm totally confused. The Rock of Rhone, Diamond Crust, Waterworks, aaaaand (SNAP FINGERS AS IF YOU'RE THINKING HARD) what was the other one? The volcano one, Magmatia, all of these four different worlds are not within one universe?"

EMPEROR: "No, no, no... they're all a part of the same universe. We're just not sure how many more universes there are... but we know for sure that the four worlds are all in the same universe...and most likely your world too."

Mr. Cape agreed with them.

AND NOW WE BEGIN THE ADVENTURES OF HELICOPTER JIM!

MR. CAPE: "Jim, I didn't know how to bring this to your attention. When I first met you, you were so new at this, and being so young I didn't want to overload you with so much information. You were lost, you were scared, you were separated from your father, and you didn't know anything. You've been learning along the way, but I have to tell you, over the time I've spent with you, you've been growing, you've been maturing, you've been getting stronger, wiser, and braver."

SCOTT: "And taller...look at him! I think he grew a couple inches…"

MR. CAPE: "Maybe it's just a part of your journey, that you're learning more and more as you go. I hope you're okay with that Jim. Don't think that we're trying to hide information from you or not being open with you. I think it's just a part of learning more and more of your calling, and who you are as you continue on your journey."

HJ: "No, it's fine. I just-- you know... it-- you're right. You know, as young as I am, and as much as I've been growing and learning, I think I can only take as much as I can at the moment. I can only receive as much as my capabilities, I guess, but I'm good with that. Yes, I'm good with that. All I know is I just want to do my very best. We can... along the way... if we have to adjust and learn, that's fine. I'm good with that."

MR. CAPE: "That's a great perspective to have. That perspective and that attitude, that maturity, is why I believe you are going to be successful in all that you do."

EMPEROR: "I agree. What can we do for you, Jim?"

HJ: "Well, I really don't know where to begin. All I know is June and September are here on Diamond Crust."

EMPEROR: "Well, my son is still here, Algoryth is still around, so you do have to be cautious of him. But we know this, we know that June and September is nowhere near us. There are other areas that you can explore. If you want, you can ask Zaiah to go with you. Zaiah is very good at locations. He's able to detect what's happening around him. He is able to read the lay of the land and able to discern what is happening with the land around him. I think he would be a good addition to your team."

Helicopter Jim looked at the team...

HJ: "What do you guys think?"

SCOTT: "I say let's take him. Any big dude like him, any big guy that we can have, I think we'll benefit from. I mean look at him he's super strong looking so that alone should intimidate anybody that comes our way. I mean we had Big Chief but if we can't have Big Chief, and Big Chief is back on the Rock of Rhone that's fine. Zaiah can come with us. I say let's take him."

Mr. Cape, Mikhail, and of course Princess Eva, were okay with taking Zaiah.

EMPEROR: "Do you guys want to stay a little while, maybe have some dinner or something?"

HJ: "You know I would love to, but I really really want to search for the Stones of June and September."

EMPEROR: "I can respect that but before you go, why don't you stock up on some food?"

HELICOPTER: "That is a good idea. Let's do that because we are running low on food and things like that."

They loaded up (HELICOPTER NAME) with various kinds of foods, fruits, meats, and of course fresh water.

After they loaded everything up, the Emperor hugged his daughter, Princess Eva, gave her a kiss on the forehead, hugged Helicopter Jim, and shook hands with the rest of the team, and bid them farewell. Helicopter Jim and the rest of the team along with Zaiah, jumped on (HELICOPTER NAME) and they sailed out of Diamond Falls. As they're sailing out, Princess Eva is waving to her father.

As they're leaving Helicopter Jim has an idea...

AND THAT WILL BE THE NEXT ADVENTURE OF HELICOPTER JIM.

Adventure 119

On the last adventure of Helicopter Jim, Mr. Cape explained to Jim that he wasn't able to tell Jim everything that is happening because there is so much information and he didn't want to burden him with so much information, especially because so many things were happening to Jim all at once.

The Emperor warned them that his son Algoryth is still looking to take the Stone of February from them, so they needed to be cautious...he also suggests that they take Zaiah with them to help locate the Stone of June and September.

EMPEROR: "Do you guys want to stay a little while, maybe have some dinner or something?"

HJ: "You know I would love to, but I really really want to search for the Stones of June and September."

EMPEROR: "I can respect that but before you go, why don't you stock up on some food?"

HELICOPTER: "That is a good idea. Let's do that because we are running low on food and things like that."

They loaded up (HELICOPTER NAME) with various kinds of foods, fruits, meats, and of course fresh water.

After they loaded everything up, the Emperor hugged his daughter, Princess Eva, gave her a kiss on the forehead, hugged Helicopter Jim, and shook hands with the rest of the team, and bid them farewell. Helicopter Jim and the rest of the team along with Zaiah, jumped on (HELICOPTER NAME) and they sailed out of Diamond Falls. As they're sailing out, Princess Eva is waving to her father.

As they're leaving Helicopter Jim has an idea...

AND NOW WE BEGIN THE ADVENTURES OF HELICOPTER JIM!

HJ: "Hey, Princess, how about this, after we retrieve the Stones of June and September, maybe we can come back and spend some time with your father and the rest of your city."

PRINCESS EVA: "I would like that. But I do agree with my father. I wasn't rescued so that I could stay home, I was rescued to come alongside you... the Chosen One, to retrieve the Stones of the Months...so I'm all in."

SCOTT: (PUMPED UP) "That's the attitude princess. That's what I want to hear because we are all in this together!"

Princess Eva rolls her eyes at Scott...

PRINCESS EVA: "I knew you'd say something like that."

So they sailed out of Diamond Falls and as they come to the other side of the falls, Zaiah senses something.

ZAIAH: "Stop. Something is not right."

Mikhail also sensed something.

MIKHAIL: "It's very heavy...dark...but not threatening...do you sense that?"

ZAIAH: "Absolutely."

And as they turned around, and looked up on the mountainside, and on the cliffs above the falls, they could see hundreds of dark shadows.

HJ: "Ummmmm...what is that? What...what are those things?"

MR. CAPE: "It's the Dark Hoods."

HJ: "What do you mean the Dark Hoods? Th-th-those are the guys that came for my dad in the museum?"

MR. CAPE: "Yes. That's them."

HJ: "So what do we-what do we do?"

MR. CAPE: "I'm not... quite... sure... yet."

ZAIAH: "I sense that they're going to attack, but they're waiting for our move first."

SCOTT: "Wait a minute, wait...so, so they're not going to attack us unless we attack them. Is that what you're saying?"

ZAIAH: "Something like that. In fact, they are unsure of us right now."

MIKHAIL: "I do sense that they are hesitant."

PRINCESS EVA: "So what do we do then?"

HELICOPTER: "I do have a count of how many there are. There are close to 500 of them, and they're not doing a thing."

SCOTT: (NERVOUSLY) "500! Yeah that kind of information, naw, you don't need to tell...you don't need to...you can keep that to yourself."

HJ: "Well, can I at least talk to them? What do I do? I don't want to just stay here, but at the same time, I don't want to just leave. What if they attack us all at once? I mean, I don't want to be caught off guard."

ZAIAH: "I think the best thing for you to do, Jim, is to see what they want. And don't worry, we're right here with you."

Helicopter Jim transformed (HELICOPTER NAME) once again into the helicopter (TRANSFORM SOUND F/X). That way at least they were protected with the surrounding of the helicopter. They flew up higher to a place where he could visibly see more of these Dark Hoods. Helicopter Jim spoke to them, and (HELICOPTER NAME) was able to project Jim's voice on the outside of the helicopter to everybody else so that they could hear.

HJ: "This is Jim. I know who you are. I know you took my father. I know you destroyed our museum, and I know you're here for me. What exactly do you want?"

Just then, one of the Dark Hoods, the leader, spoke up. He was carrying a staff with a blue crystal on the end of it. He asked a question…

AND THAT WILL BE THE NEXT ADVENTURE OF HELICOPTER JIM.

Adventure 120

On the last adventure of Helicopter Jim, Jim, Mikhail, Princess Eva, Scott, Mr. Cape, and Zaiah headed out of Diamond Falls to search for the Stones of June and September.

On the way out, Zaiah and Mikhail sensed that something wasn't right...they realized that they were surrounded by 500 Dark Hoods. They were unsure of why they were there. The good news was that at least they weren't being attacked by them. They just didn't know what to do...

ZAIAH: "I think the best thing for you to do, Jim, is to see what they want. Don't worry, we're right here with you."

Helicopter Jim transformed (HELICOPTER NAME) once again into the helicopter. That way at least they were protected with the surrounding of the helicopter. They flew up higher to a place where he could visibly see more of these Dark Hoods. Helicopter Jim spoke to them, and (HELICOPTER NAME) was able to project Jim's voice on the outside of the helicopter to everybody else so that they could hear.

HJ: "This is Jim. I know who you are. I know you took my father. I know you destroyed our museum, and I know you're here for me. What exactly do you want?"

Just then, one of the Dark Hoods, the leader, spoke up. He was carrying a staff with a blue crystal on the end of it. He asked a question...

AND NOW WE BEGIN THE ADVENTURES OF HELICOPTER JIM!

DH LEADER: "Do you have the Stone of January?"

HJ: "What are you talking about?"

Once again, the leader of the Dark Hoods asked...

DH LEADER: "Do you have the Stone of January?"

HJ: (SARCASTICALLY) "What is this, 'Stone of January?' Why do you need to know if I have this... Stone?"

DH LEADER: "Because if you do have January, then you are the Chosen One, and if you are the Chosen One, we need to know."

HJ: "What kind of reasoning is that? Why should I tell you if I have the Stone of January? Just so that you can attack us and try to take it away?"

DH LEADER: "If that's your reasoning, and if that's your answer, Jim, then, obviously, you have the Stone of January."

Helicopter Jim looked at everyone, Scott looked at Jim...

SCOTT: "Even I could have done better than that Jim! Come on!"

MR. CAPE: "Jim, just tell them the truth. If they're going to attack, then let them attack. We'll be ready for them."

HJ: "Are you all sure? If I do this...we're all in danger."

Everyone was ready for whatever might happen...

HJ: "Okay...here I go..."

Jim then courageously responds to the leader of the Dark Hoods...

HJ: "I absolutely have the Stone of January."

DH LEADER: "Then it is accurate. You are the Chosen One."

HJ: (WITH SARCASM) "That's what they keep telling me, that I'm the Chosen One. And because I'm the Chosen One, there are many things that I need to accomplish, so you are wasting my time. Let me know what you need, what you want. If I can accomplish it, great. If not, then I need to leave. I don't want to be around the people who took my father. Wherever you took him, I will find him."

DH LEADER: "We can understand your frustration and your anger, but you have everything wrong."

HJ: "It's not I who have things wrong, it's what you guys are doing that makes everything wrong. You didn't even ask questions. All you did was come in and take my father. You took him away from me."

MR. CAPE: "Hey, Jim, take it easy a little. I know you're emotional right now because they took your father, but we need to focus."

HJ: "No, no, they took my dad, so I want to know where my dad is, where they took him to."

DH LEADER: "This is not the time and place to talk about it, Jim."

HJ: "This is the time and place, right here, right now. You let me know where my father is, or I will attack you!"

DH LEADER: "Jim, this is not the time and place."

ZAIAH: "Jim, there's something you need to know."

MIKHAIL: "I don't know what it is Jim, but I don't think they're here to attack you."

HJ: "What do you mean they're not here to attack me? Why would they come all this way and wait for me to come out of Diamond Falls if they didn't want to attack me?"

ZAIAH: "Because they would have attacked you by now."

HJ: "I don't get it. Why are you guys even here?"

DH LEADER: "Let's talk about this somewhere else. Follow us."

HJ: "Follow you? What do you mean follow you? I'm not falling into any one of your traps."

DH LEADER: "If you want to see your father, follow us."

Then, all of a sudden...

AND THAT WILL BE THE NEXT ADVENTURE OF HELICOPTER JIM.

Adventure 121

On the last adventure of Helicopter Jim, the leader of the Dark Hoods questioned Jim if he had the Stone of January. After having a tough time trusting the leader, Jim eventually told him he had the Stone.

The leader wants to discuss something with Jim, but Jim is frustrated and doesn't want to waste any more time speaking with the leader of the Dark Hoods, so Jim threatened to attack him if he didn't let him know where his father was...

MIKHAIL: "I don't know what it is Jim, but I don't think they're here to attack you."

HJ: "What do you mean they're not here to attack me? Why would they come all this way and wait for me to come out of Diamond Falls if they didn't want to attack me?"

ZAIAH: "Because they would have attacked you by now."

HJ: "I don't get it. Why are you even here?"

DH LEADER: "Let's talk about this somewhere else. Follow us."

HJ: "Follow you? What do you mean follow you? I'm not falling into any one of your traps."

DH LEADER: "If you want to see your father, follow us."

Then, all of a sudden...

AND NOW WE BEGIN THE ADVENTURES OF HELICOPTER JIM!

Then, all of a sudden, the leader of the Dark Hoods shot up

into the sky, and so did all the other Dark Hoods.

HJ: "I guess we're following them."

They followed the Dark Hoods all the way, as high as they could go. They went so high that they could no longer see Diamond Falls. As they're heading up into the sky, they go through all of the clouds, and they are now high up into the sky. As they go higher into the sky, Helicopter Jim notices that the Dark Hoods are now in a weird formation. They're all spread out, and then they turn around and wait for Jim to catch up. Now they're all in the sky, and Helicopter Jim addresses the leader of the Dark Hoods…

HJ: "Where's my father?"

DH LEADER: "We're going to need to go through to the other side."

HJ: "What do you mean through to the other side?"

DH LEADER: "Yes, your father is on the other side."

HJ: "What do you mean on the other side, the other side of what?"

DH LEADER: "The other side of the barrier."

HJ: "What do you mean barrier? What barrier?"

DH LEADER: "Right behind me is a barrier, and that's where your father is. That was the safest place for him to be."

HJ: "What do you mean the safest place? The safest place for what? Why are you putting him in a safe place? You're the ones who took him."

DH LEADER: "We had to. The only way to protect your

father was to get him first before Dayor did."

HJ: "I don't understand. What do you mean?"

DH LEADER: "Dayor found out where your father was."

HJ: "What do you mean he found out where my father was, so you guys... you're telling me you came in to take my father so that he wouldn't be taken by Dayor?"

DH LEADER: "That is absolutely correct. This barrier that separates us from your father, is a one way in, once, for one person. Your father cannot get out and no one can go in... except one person..."

HJ: "Let me guess, the Chosen One."

DH LEADER: "You are correct. Jim, only you can go through the barrier."

Helicopter Jim didn't know what to do. He didn't know if he could trust the leader of the Dark Hoods.

He didn't know if...if he went through the barrier, if it was a trap, if it was going to be a prison. He was trying to learn from what happened with the Queen's sister when he was trapped in the vault. And he didn't know what to do.

PRINCESS EVA: "Jim, you're going to have to make a difficult decision."

HJ: "What if he's, what if he's lying though and...and...and, I go in there, and then I'm stuck there forever. I, I don't know if I can trust these guys. Remember, now I'm not supposed to trust anybody."

PRINCESS EVA: "Do you trust you? Can you trust that

being the Chosen One, that you're going to find a way to make it work… because it's…it's…it's… going to be on you anyway, Jim. We can all help you, we can be here to support you, but ultimately, you're going to have to make the tough decisions."

MIKHAIL: "I agree Jim, we're all here to support you. You're just going to have to make the decision."

So Jim grabbed the Stone of January for Wisdom. And as Jim thought it through with the Stone of January, wisdom said to proceed and go through the barrier.

HJ: "(HELICOPTER NAME), I'm going to go through the barrier. If I don't come back, then please take care of my friends."

HELICOPTER: "You'll be back Jim. You will be fine… after all… you are… the Chosen One."

AND THAT WILL BE THE NEXT ADVENTURE OF HELICOPTER JIM.

Adventure 122

On the last adventure of Helicopter Jim, the Dark Hoods led Helicopter Jim high up into the sky...so high that they no longer could see Diamond Falls.

The leader of the Dark Hoods led Jim and the team to the barrier where Jim's dad was kept. The only person who could go through the barrier was the Chosen One. But Jim didn't trust the leader...he needed wisdom...

So Jim grabbed the Stone of January for Wisdom. And as he thought it through with the Stone of January, wisdom said to proceed and go through the barrier.

HJ: "(HELICOPTER NAME), I'm going to go through the barrier. If I don't come back, then please take care of my friends."

HELICOPTER: "You'll be back Jim. You will be fine… after all… you are… the Chosen One."

AND NOW WE BEGIN THE ADVENTURES OF HELICOPTER JIM!

Helicopter Jim approached the barrier and stood in front of it. He was about to cross through and all of a sudden he hears something...something loud...it is the cry of an eagle. He hears a screeching sound. (SCREECHING SOUND LIKE AN EAGLE) And he's wondering…

HJ: "What is that?"

Helicopter Jim turns around and off in the faint distance he sees a shiny yellow glow and it is coming toward him, growing bigger and bigger at a fast rate.

Helicopter Jim is wondering if that's a part of going through the barrier. Did he trigger something? Is it because he's going to go through the barrier and cross through it, that something is being triggered? As he's thinking this through, he looks at the bright yellow glow and it is actually a fireball coming his way.

HELICOPTER: "Jim, you're going to have to act quickly!"

HJ: "I know but what is that? What is that coming our way?"

HELICOPTER: "Don't worry about it. Just go through the barrier."

HJ: "But what...what...what is that? I don't want to go through the barrier and something happens to the barrier and I'm stuck there. What is that?"

HELICOPTER: "Don't worry. Just go through. You must go through now!"

HJ: "No, I can't. I need to know what that is."

MR. CAPE: (WITH URGENCY) "Jim, don't worry. You need to get through to the barrier. You need to see your father. You need to go to the other side!"

HJ: "No. I'm not going to leave you guys. What if you're in harm's way? In fact, that looks like a fireball coming our way. I'm not going to leave you guys out here to be destroyed."

HELICOPTER: "Jim, what you see coming our way is not a fireball. It is fury, the Fire Eagle."

HJ: "Fury! Soooo... is that good or bad? Wh..what is that?"

MIKHAIL: "It is not good. Fury is relentless in his attacks.

He will not give up until we are all destroyed. So either you go through the barrier and be safe or we all will be destroyed. At least you can go through to the other side and be safe."

HJ: "I'm not going to leave you guys."

PRINCESS EVA: (BRAVELY) "Then we all will stand and fight."

ZAIAH: "I have your sword Princess...just give me the word."

SCOTT: "What do you mean, we all will stand and fight? Is that it? Just because Fury is coming our way. That's our only option? Wait...what? Sword? You have a sword Princess?"

HJ: "Well, I'm not leaving you guys. I'm not going to the other side of the barrier. I say we stand and fight. What does Fury want anyway?"

MIKHAIL: "Fury will stop at nothing until we are destroyed. We are a threat to him."

HJ: "What do you mean we're a threat? What…what...what...do you know that I don't know?"

MIKHAIL: "Fury was created for one reason, for one thing. He has one mission and that is all he was created for."

HJ: "Well, wh...what is the mission?"

MR. CAPE: "We're so sorry Jim, we didn't know how to tell you earlier when we saw Fury while retrieving August...But his mission… is to destroy the Chosen One… and he will stop at nothing until that happens. Jim, you need to go to the other side of the barrier. You'll be safe. Don't worry about us. We'll be okay."

HJ: "That's not good enough. There has to be another way. There has to be a way for us to...to stand and fight and do something."

MIKHAIL: "There's nothing we can do. We cannot defeat Fury."

HJ: "I say we can. Let's stand and fight. I have the Stones... I'll use the Stones."

Helicopter Jim grabs January. He holds it in his hand and as he does, he uses wisdom, strength of the mind. He thinks to himself, what can he do to defeat Fury?

All of a sudden…

AND THAT WILL BE THE NEXT ADVENTURE OF HELICOPTER JIM.

Adventure 123

On the last adventure of Helicopter Jim, just before Jim entered the barrier to see his father, they hear a loud screech from Fury, the Fire Eagle.

Everyone wanted Jim to see his father, so they encouraged him to enter the barrier...but Jim did not want to leave them. He learned that Fury had a mission, one mission only, and that was to destroy the Chosen One. Jim chose to stay and fight...

MIKHAIL: "There's nothing we can do. We cannot defeat Fury."

HJ: "I say we can. Let's stand and fight. I have the Stones... I'll use the Stones."

Helicopter Jim grabs January. He holds it in his hand and as he does, he uses wisdom, strength of the mind. He thinks to himself, what can he do to defeat Fury?

All of a sudden...

AND NOW WE BEGIN THE ADVENTURES OF HELICOPTER JIM!

All of a sudden...Jim remembers the Stone of June, which brings Blue the giant Eagle to life.

HJ: "Wait a minute. Mikhail, what if we were to get June and...and...and look for Blue the Giant Eagle?"

MIKHAIL: "What do you mean look for the Giant Eagle? For what?"

HJ: "To defeat Fury. Maybe we have a fighting chance with

Blue."

MR. CAPE: "We're going to have to make a decision quickly. Fury is soon to be here."

They can still see in the faint distance that Fury is on his way because it's getting bigger and bigger. It's only a matter of seconds until Fury is right where they are.

HJ: "I say let's look for Blue. But we need to retrieve the Stone of June first. And according to the 12 Pillars, June is right here on Diamond Crust. So I say let's look for June."

HELICOPTER: "Well, you're going to have to move quickly because Fury is right there. We need to move quickly."

HJ: "Let's go. Let's look for June and let's see if we can get out of Fury's reach."

They all jump in (HELICOPTER NAME).

HELICOPTER: "Everyone hang on tightly. We need to move!"

(HELICOPTER NAME) takes off quickly and uses its boosters to get them out of Fury's reach, and they speed their way out of that area. Fury cannot reach them. They got out of there in time.

PRINCESS EVA: "Now where do we go Jim? How do we know where the Stone of June is?"

HJ: "I don't know. I really don't."

As they're flying through the air Jim remembers the Dark Hoods and the leader. Maybe the leader would know.

HJ: "Why don't we turn around and ask the leader of the

Dark Hoods? They may know something."

HELICOPTER NAME: "We're going to turn around? Fury is there."

HJ: "Well, we...we have to somehow find a way to retrieve June, so we're going to have to face Fury one way or the other."

Helicopter Jim decides to turn around and he goes back to the area where Fury is. And sure enough, Fury is where they were by the barrier, but the leader of the Dark Hoods is nowhere to be seen.

HELICOPTER: "They're not in this area, but I can detect where they are. And I can take us there. I know where they are."

(HELICOPTER NAME) locates the leader of the Dark Hoods and within minutes he is able to get to where the Dark Hoods are.

They are in a faraway place, far from Diamond Falls.

HELICOPTER: "Jim, the Dark Hoods are in that forest area, that swampy area. We're going to have to go there."

So as they're flying over the area, Zaiah notices something...

ZAIAH: "This is the Swamplands Beyond...it's a very tricky place...be careful."

HJ: "Thanks Zaiah. Well, let's go then. Let's go look for them."

AND THAT WILL BE THE NEXT ADVENTURE OF HELICOPTER JIM.

Adventure 124

On the last adventure of Helicopter Jim, Jim decides to look for Blue, the Giant Eagle and suggests that they look for the leader of the Dark Hoods to ask if he knows where they might find the Stone of June. Fury is coming closer to them so (HELICOPTER NAME) quickly gets them out of danger and now they are very far from Fury. (HELICOPTER NAME) is able to track down and locate where the Dark Hoods are...

They are in a faraway place, far from Diamond Falls.

HELICOPTER: "Jim, the Dark Hoods are in that forest area, that swampy area. We're going to have to go there."

So as they're flying over the area, Zaiah notices something...

ZAIAH: "This is the Swamplands Beyond...it's a very tricky place...be careful."

HJ: "Thanks Zaiah. Well, let's go then. Let's go look for them."

AND NOW WE BEGIN THE ADVENTURES OF HELICOPTER JIM.

(HELICOPTER NAME) slowly descends upon this dark, gloomy, cold, and wet forest swamp area and Helicopter Jim transforms the helicopter into this massive boat so that they can float down into the swamp. It's not a boat like the kind of boat you would be in a river with. It's a different kind of boat, one that can go through a swamp. They're still protected being inside (HELICOPTER NAME) but still able to float in the swamps, and they're slowly navigating through the swamps.

SCOTT: "Do we know where we're going?"

HELICOPTER: "Yes. Do you see that blue dot on the Trxsol?"

SCOTT: "Yes. I do."

HELICOPTER: "That's where we're heading. That's where the Dark Hoods are, but we need to proceed slowly because we have no idea what's in this area."

As they proceed towards the area where the Dark Hoods are, they're still mindful that Fury is out there. They don't want to do anything sudden that would attract Fury.

HJ: "Well, once we get to the leader, hopefully they're able to help us with the Stone of June."

As they're getting closer to the blue dot on the Trxsol, Mikhail senses something...

MIKHAIL: "Jim, we are not safe right here where we are."

HELICOPTER: "I was just about to say that."

MIKHAIL: "You sense something too?"

HELICOPTER: "Yes, I do. I have no idea what it is, but there is something beneath this swamp. Something massive."

SCOTT: "What do you mean something massive? Is this...is this...is this good or bad? What...what...what are you...what are you sensing?"

HELICOPTER: "I sense something massive. In fact, I can detect that there's something underneath the water."

MIKHAIL: "I sense it too. It's not dangerous but it's not

friendly either. There's just something under this water."

MR. CAPE: "Well, whatever it is we're going to have to do something. Either we go quicker and get to where that blue dot is or we're going to face the consequences of whatever you guys are sensing."

SCOTT: "Well, whatever you're sensing, we..we have to do something. I don't..I don't want anything to happen to us. We... we shouldn't wait for anything. We should get to that blue dot as quickly as possible."

As Scott was speaking, all of a sudden the waters start to bubble, starts to look like boiling water. It's not hot, there's just bubbles popping up. It seems like there's something under the water.

HJ: "What is that? What is happening?"

HELICOPTER: "I'm not sure what that is. I have no idea what that is, but there is definitely something under the water. It's not alive, there's just something there."

All of a sudden, the whole entire swamp is raging with bubbles. It is so fierce that it begins to rock (HELICOPTER NAME) and it's tossing them, left and right, up and down and everybody's being shaken inside (HELICOPTER NAME).

HJ: "Everybody hang on. Buckle up!"

And they're trying to get to their seats but the waters are raging and rapid and so uncontrollable that they are having a hard time standing still. (HELICOPTER NAME) is being tossed all over the place. It is a strong thing that is happening with the waters bubbling.

And then out of nowhere…

AND THAT WILL BE THE NEXT ADVENTURE OF HELICOPTER JIM.

Adventure 125

On the last adventure of Helicopter Jim, (HELICOPTER NAME) is able to pinpoint the location of the Dark Hoods. They are in this dark, gloomy, swamp area, so Jim transforms (HELICOPTER NAME) into a boat that is able to go through the swamp, but still able to protect them...

HJ: "What is that? What is happening?"

HELICOPTER: "I'm not sure what that is. I have no idea what that is, but there is definitely something under the water. It's not alive, there's just something there."

All of a sudden, the whole entire swamp is raging with bubbles. It is so fierce that it begins to rock (HELICOPTER NAME) and it's tossing them, left and right, up and down and everybody's being shaken inside (HELICOPTER NAME).

HJ: "Everybody hang on. Buckle up!"

And they're trying to get to their seats but the waters are raging and rapid and so uncontrollable that they are having a hard time standing still. (HELICOPTER NAME) is being tossed all over the place. It is a strong thing that is happening with the waters bubbling.

And then out of nowhere...

AND NOW WE BEGIN THE ADVENTURES OF HELICOPTER JIM!

Out of nowhere, the entire swamp is swallowed up underground and they all are sucked into this massive sinkhole. And they get pulled under the water and into this huge area and they drop down into the sinkhole. (CRASHING SOUND F/X) They crash and they land in this huge sinkhole. Now, they're underneath this entire swamp area and as they look up, they are underneath the swamp, not underwater...they're just separated and they are on this thick area of mud. They're stuck in this mud.

HELICOPTER: "This is some sticky mud!"

HJ: "Well...I, I'm going to have to… let me… I'm going to have to change you into a helicopter so that we can get out of here. What just happened?"

HELICOPTER: "We were taken underneath the swamp. We are under the swamp right now!"

And as they look around, everything is dark.

HELICOPTER: "The bad news is we just got sucked under the swamp and I have no idea where we are exactly, but there is good news!"

SCOTT: "I like that. What is the good news?"

HELICOPTER: "We are right on the blue dot."

HJ: "Well, that's good then. Wh..wh..where are they? Where are the...the Dark Hoods?"

HELICOPTER: "I detect them. I just can't see them."

HJ: (YELLING) "Where are you guys!? We know you're here. Where are you guys?"

And all of a sudden, Helicopter Jim sees a tiny, tiny blue glow in the distance and the tiny blue glow gets brighter and brighter and is coming closer to Jim.

HELICOPTER: "Do you see that blue glow coming your

way?"

HJ: "Yes."

HELICOPTER: "That's the leader of the Dark Hoods."

HJ: "Then why can't I see him?"

HELICOPTER: "Because right now, he is blending in with the dark."

The blue dot gets closer and closer, it's a blue glow. And now, the blue glow is right in front of Helicopter Jim...

HJ: "Are...is...is that you? Is..is that you?"

DH LEADER: "Yes, it is.,"

HJ: "Why didn't you say something? Why didn't you even-- Why did we have to go through all of this just to find you guys and...and...and why didn't you say anything when we got here?"

DH LEADER: "Because Fury can detect us that easily, so we have to be careful that we do not do things that capture his attention. Otherwise, he would know where you are too. Fury is very good at finding *you*. That's what he was created for. He will continuously hunt you down. So we have to be mindful of what he is doing. That was a close one back there by the barrier. Why didn't you go through?"

HJ: "Because everyone was in danger. There's no way I was going to go through and just save myself."

DH LEADER: "Fury knows where the barrier is now and he knows that you need to go through it."

HJ: "Well, my thought is I...I...I, I need...I need to retrieve the Stone of June."

DH LEADER: "You're going for Blue, aren't you?"

HJ: "How did you know?"

DH LEADER: "Because that's the wise thing to do."

HJ: "Do you know where the Stone of June is?"

DH LEADER: "No. I have no idea where June is, but there is a way for you to detect where June is."

HJ: "How will I know?"

DH LEADER: "This staff that I hold, once given to you, will lead you to the Stone of June."

HJ: "Why don't you-- Why are you telling me this now? Why didn't you...why didn't you just tell me this earlier? Why didn't you give this to me earlier?"

DH LEADER: "Because *you* needed to know that you needed Blue. It's not something that I can tell you. Although you need help along the way, there are just certain things no one can tell you. There are many things you're just going to have to figure out yourself and we cannot get in the way. Otherwise, we jeopardize your mission, but since you decided to search for Blue, I can hand over the staff that will lead you there."

The leader hands Jim his staff with this blue crystal on the end of it. Jim takes a hold of it and feels a power come over him, (POWER SOUND F/X).

SCOTT: "Whoa, whoa, whoa, whoa, whoa, what was that?"

HJ: "I have no idea."

MR. CAPE: "That, Jim, was just a glimpse of the kind of power that you'll receive when you retrieve the Stone of June."

AND THAT WILL BE THE NEXT ADVENTURE OF HELICOPTER JIM.

Adventure 126

On the last adventure of Helicopter Jim, as (HELICOPTER NAME) was taking them through the swamp, all of a sudden they dropped into this enormous sinkhole and found themselves under the swamp.

Helicopter Jim was met with the leader of the Dark Hoods and learned from the leader that they needed to be cautious because Fury can easily find them.

The leader of the Dark Hoods asked Jim if he was in search of Blue and if he was, there was a way to find the Stone of June, which is needed to bring Blue the Giant Eagle to life...

The leader hands Jim his staff with this blue crystal on the end of it. Jim takes a hold of it and feels a power come over him, (POWER SOUND F/X).

SCOTT: "Whoa, whoa, whoa, whoa, whoa, what was that?"

HJ: "I have no idea."

MR. CAPE: "That, Jim, was just a glimpse of the kind of power that you'll receive when you retrieve the Stone of June."

AND NOW WE BEGIN THE ADVENTURES OF HELICOPTER JIM!

As Jim was about to leave, the leader of the Dark Hoods had one more thing for Jim...

DH LEADER: "Come with me, all of you...I want to introduce you to some people. I think they'll come in handy."

The leader led them to a place that was deep below the

swamps. He entered a place that was very dark and cold.

HJ: "Where are we going, why is it so cold?"

DH LEADER: "Because we are very deep below the surface of the swamp. These people that I'm going to introduce you to, will help you along your journey. There's something you need to understand about these people that I'm going to introduce you to."

HJ: "Um, are they going to- are they going to, what do you mean, um, help me along...along the journey? They're- they're- they're coming with us? They're coming with me, or what do you mean, help me along the journey?"

DH LEADER: "Well, that's the thing, they're able to be with you, but you won't know they're around."

HJ: "What do you mean 'They won't know,' I won't know they're around? How can I... how can I not know they're around? Aren't you going... going to be with me? If they're along with me for the journey, why wouldn't I know they're around?"

DH LEADER: "Because these guys are stealth. They're so stealth that even I have a hard time finding them. Come, let's enter into this area right here."

The leader of the Dark Hoods took Helicopter Jim through this canal underground. And it was a small area where there was what felt like water.

HJ: "Where-where are we going, why-why is there water under here? That's kind of weird, is there... is there water coming from the swamp?"

DH LEADER: "No, that's not water that's just the density of

how cold it is. It feels like water, but there's nothing there."

As they entered into this one room, this room was filled with various kinds of different odd shapes. But because it was dark, they could hardly see.

DH LEADER: "Can I borrow that?"

Helicopter Jim gave him the staff. And he held up the staff, and it shot light to various areas and lit up different crystals... all in shades of blue... light blue, dark blue, bright blue, all different shades of blue. And it lit up the entire room, and Helicopter Jim looked around and could see, he could see all of these different types of gadgets and various inventions.

HJ: "What is this place?"

DH LEADER: "This is the imagination room."

HJ: "What is- what does that mean imagination room? You... you... this is where you come to think about things?"

DH LEADER: "No, this is not where-where I come to think about things. This is where they come to think about things."

HJ: "Who... who's they, what do you mean they?"

DH LEADER: "I want to introduce you to JD, Little Oak, and here is... El lando."

HJ: "Oh... I don't see any of them, where are they?"

DH LEADER: "They're standing right in front of you."

And all of a sudden...

AND THAT WILL BE THE NEXT ADVENTURE OF HELICOPTER JIM.

Adventure 127

On the last adventure of Helicopter Jim, the leader of the Dark Hoods took Helicopter Jim, Scott, Princess Eva, Mikhail, Mr. Cape and Zaiah to a room filled with different gadgets and various inventions.

DH LEADER: "This is the imagination room."

HJ: "What is- what does that mean imagination room? You... you... this is where you come to think about things?"

DH LEADER: "No, this is not where-where I come to think about things. This is where they come to think about things."

HJ: "Who... who's they, what do you mean they?"

DH LEADER: "I want to introduce you to JD, Little Oak, and here is... El lando."

HJ: "Oh... I don't see any of them, where are they?"

DH LEADER: "They're standing right in front of you."

And all of a sudden...

AND NOW WE BEGIN THE ADVENTURES OF HELICOPTER JIM!

And all of a sudden, Helicopter Jim hears laughter, and all three of them are laughing. Helicopter Jim can't even see them, but he hears them laughing. (SNICKERING LAUGHTER)

HJ: "What is that? Why can't I see them?"

DH LEADER: "Because they're not wanting you to see them. Guys come on, can we just at least show up and make yourself known."

Then all of a sudden, right in front of Helicopter Jim, appears these three men.

HJ: (STARTLED) "Whoa, where'd you come from...how'd you do that?"

JD: "This is how we...we can be stealth at any time. This here is my brother El Lando, and that's my younger brother Little Oak. We're here to help you achieve success on your journey and with your mission to retrieve the stones."

DH LEADER: "This is Jim, they call him Helicopter Jim...he is...the Chosen One."

HJ: "Would you guys... you guys look kind of young for what you're about to do, you look kind of young to help me on my journey... except of course for you Little Oak. What-what-what are you guys gonna do?"

JD: "Young! We're a lot older than you! We just look young."

HJ: "Well, how old are you? What are you 10, 12, 13?"

JD: "That's so funny, I'm over 1,100 years old."

HJ: "1,000 years! (CHUCKLES) You know that... you can't be 1,000 years old? How can you be 1,000 years old? No one lives for 1,000 years."

JD: "1,100... and you're looking at one. And my other two brothers... El Lando, how old are you El Lando?

EL LANDO: "I am 900 years old, a little over give or take a couple of years."

LITTLE OAK: "Yup, and I just turned 700 years old."

HJ: "Your name is 'Little Oak' and yet you're super huge!"

JD: "Yeah, for some reason...he just kept growing. We're... we're 200 years apart, that's just how it is, but let's get on to the good stuff. Come, let me show you something."

JD took Helicopter Jim into this other room. The leader of the Dark Hoods handed Jim the staff back...

DH LEADER: "I call them 'The Mighty 3.' Good luck you guys. And hey guys, take care of Jim, you know what to do."

THE MIGHTY 3: "We will...got it."

JD: "First of all, we're going to have to equip you with the best of the best equipment. Let's see what we got. Let's equip you with some gadgets that will help you along the way. El Lando, help him with battle gear. Little Oak, get him some gadgets."

EL LANDO: "Okay, what kind of gear do you want? Do you want hand-to-hand combat? Do you want stealth? What do you want?"

HJ: "I don't... I don't know what... what... whatever is best, I don't know what... what should I have?"

LITTLE OAK: "Well, you probably have friends with you too, so you're gonna wanna equip them also."

EL LANDO: "Oh yes, you're gonna want to equip them too, so here's what I'll do. Let me equip you first, stock you up, and then we can go to each person after you... Okay for you Jim, you definitely will want this sword. This sword is amazing. I call it... Legend."

HJ: "A Legendary sword!? What do you mean... Legend?"

EL LANDO: "Little Oak, explain to Helicopter Jim. What this is."

LITTLE OAK: "Okay, this is one of my best inventions. This sword has within its capabilities what you know as nuclear power. So every time you strike the sword, it unleashes the same type of power as a small nuclear burst. When you strike someone else's sword, or whatever it comes in contact with, power is generated through their sword, or the item they're using, and will definitely knock them out, or destroy whatever it strikes...or at least cause major damage."

HJ: "Wait...wait...if it's able to generate that much power, what about me? How...how do I get protected? What if...what if I get...what if… isn't it going to affect me too?"

LITTLE OAK: "No, that's...that's what's so special about this sword. The special design of the handle absorbs the hit too. Also, I have here for your side pouch... I have these little spikes. These little spikes are just in case you find yourself in a...in a tough situation and you're not able to swing your sword. You can throw these little spikes and as they hit the target it will...once it gets stuck into the target...it explodes as if they got hit by the sword. You're gonna love it!"

HJ: "Okay, I...I'll...I'll take that, that's fine."

JD: "What about his armor El Lando? Get him some armor?"

EL LANDO: "Okay, this armor is going to be your best armor. But you're going to have to choose. Would you rather your armor have flexibility? Or do you want your armor to be strong, which may require a little bit of heaviness?"

HJ: "Uh, I don't know, uh, ummm, if it's flexible, I can move, more... right? But would I still be protected?"

EL LANDO: "Yes, you'll still be protected."

HJ: "Well, I'll...I'll take that one... I'll take flexibility over heaviness. I don't want to be weighed down."

LITTLE OAK: "Or what we can do El Lando, is we can ready him up with The Final Cloak."

JD: "The Final Cloak isn't ready yet."

LITTLE OAK: "It is ready, I just haven't field tested it yet."

HJ: "Wait a minute. I'm not going to use something you have not tested yet."

LITTLE OAK: "Just... you're gonna...you're gonna...you're gonna want this cloak. The Final Cloak is...is...is good because you have both flexibility and strength, plus durability. And at the same time, watch this."

AND THAT WILL BE THE NEXT ADVENTURE OF HELICOPTER JIM!

Adventure 128

On the last adventure of Helicopter Jim, they were introduced to the Mighty 3. The Mighty 3 equipped Jim with Legend, a nuclear battle sword. Jim needed to decide for his armor if he wanted flexibility or strength.

Little Oak suggested that JD equip Helicopter Jim with The Final Cloak…

JD: "The Final Cloak isn't ready yet."

LITTLE OAK: "It is ready, I just haven't field tested it yet."

HJ: "Wait a minute. I'm not going to use something you have not tested yet."

LITTLE OAK: (SOUND CONVINCING) "Just... you're gonna...you're gonna...you're gonna want this cloak. The Final Cloak is...is...is good because you have both flexibility and strength, plus durability. And at the same time, watch this."

AND NOW WE BEGIN THE ADVENTURES OF HELICOPTER JIM!

Little Oak threw the cloak over himself… and disappeared.

HJ: (AMAZED) "What? I'll take that. That one, yes, definitely."

And so Little Oak took The Final Cloak and gave it to Helicopter Jim.

And so Helicopter Jim had Legend, the Nuke Sword, little spikes, and The Final Cloak.

HJ: "This is amazing. Thank you. I appreciate it.

This...this...this would be good for me. I mean, no matter where I go, I feel like I'm...I'm much more protected now."

JD: "What about your other friends? What...what can we equip them with?"

So Helicopter Jim called everybody and they all came down and El Lando equipped them all.

EL LANDO: Scott, I'm going to equip you with a crossbow. I call it, The InvisiBow, a special crossbow. It isn't just any crossbow, it is invisible and shoots invisible arrows. No one can see these except you. And you too will be equipped with The Final Cloak. For you Mikhail, you'll be equipped with the power staff and liquid metal as your armor. Mr. Cape, You will be equipped with a state of the art bow and arrow. But don't be fooled, this is not the normal bow and arrow. This bow was made with a modified special metal grade material that is unbreakable and can withstand the most extreme temperatures, which is why I call it, the UnbreakaBow. It is equipped with arrows that are stronger than any metal we know of and because these arrows are molecularly made, it uses resources from its surroundings, therefore, your arrows will never run out, but it does dissolve within a few seconds. Oh... and these arrows... are smart arrows. Wherever you need them to go, all you need to do is direct them. And for your armor... The Infinite Breastplate, which is able to protect your entire body. With one press of this button, your whole body will be covered with armor that will protect you. Princess, because you already have a sword, take the rope chain and the ring of protection...

PRINCESS EVA: "How do you know I have a sword?"

EL LANDO: "Because we made it for you when you were born."

PRINCESS EVA: "Really!? Wow...I love my sword! Thank you!"

EL LANDO: "Here, put the ring on any finger...it'll self fit. Zaiah, because of your size and strength, take The Power Sword as well as The Shield of Absorption, which means that anything that hits the shield will be absorbed into the shield."

So everybody was equipped.

HJ: "This is amazing. I can't thank you guys enough. And also...uhhh, you know, your...your leader said that you were able to come with us on the journey. I don't...I don't know how...how... that's gonna happen. I mean, what...what do you guys want me to do? I mean, are you gonna come with us? What do you...what do you want to do?"

JD: "No, we'll...we'll be with you. I mean, now that you have these, now that you're equipped, we'll be with you all the way through the journey, we'll always be with you."

HJ: "How...how is that possible? Like, are you coming with us into, uh, my helicopter, or what?"

EL LANDO: "No, you don't understand... because you have all of our gear, we will always be with you. It's just the way it is. No matter where you are, we are always there with you. So if you need anything, we're here."

HJ: "Man, too bad I can't take all of these things with me. Look at all of this gear you have!"

JD: "But that's the point. We'll be with you. And because

we're with you, all of these...all of this equipment is at your disposal at any time. So if you need any gear-any of this gear, you just need to let us know. The gear that we just equipped you with, will always be with you. So you can take that with you."

HJ: "That's...that's amazing. I don't...I don't understand how that works but I'm okay with it."

And so Helicopter Jim and the rest of the team left that area. They thanked The Mighty 3, JD, El Lando, and Little Oak for helping them with being equipped for what lay ahead.

As they left that area Helicopter Jim had the staff with the crystal, the blue crystal on it…

HJ: "The Darkhood's leader gave me this staff with this crystal on the end of it and he said this will lead us to the Stone of June, so let's go, let's...let's see where it leads us."

AND THAT WILL BE THE NEXT ADVENTURE OF HELICOPTER JIM.

Adventure 129

On the last adventure of Helicopter Jim, after Jim and the rest of the team were equipped with battle gear, Helicopter Jim was hoping that The Mighty 3 would be able to come with them to find the rest of the Stones.

JD: "But that's the point. We'll be with you. And because we're with you, all of these...all of this equipment is at your disposal at any time. So if you need any gear-any of this gear, you just need to let us know. The gear that we just equipped you with, will always be with you. So you can take that with you."

HJ: "That's...that's amazing. I don't...I don't understand how that works but I'm okay with it."

And so Helicopter Jim and the rest of the team left that area. They thanked The Mighty 3, JD, El Lando, and Little Oak for helping them with being equipped for what lay ahead.

As they left that area Helicopter Jim had the staff with the crystal, the blue crystal on it…

HJ: "The Darkhood's leader gave me this staff with this crystal on the end of it and he said this will lead us to the Stone of June, so let's go, let's...let's see where it leads us."

AND NOW WE BEGIN THE ADVENTURES OF HELICOPTER JIM!

And the staff pulled Jim. It guided them, it pulled at Helicopter Jim in different directions. So as he entered into (HELICOPTER NAME) as Jim was thinking of where to fly, (HELICOPTER NAME) was able to connect with Jim's thoughts.

HELICOPTER: "I got it Jim. I know where it is. The staff is guiding you in your thoughts. And I can sense where it's pulling you to. And I have an idea of where the Stone may be."

So they all entered into (HELICOPTER NAME) and exited the swamp area. And as they're flying, they notice that they're heading into an area where there are various kinds of rocks and mountains and it looks like a place that was empty and void of life... devastated by earthquakes. So, (HELICOPTER NAME) slowly lands in this area that was clear, free from anything.

HJ: "Is this where we have to go? Because, uh, this place looks familiar. It just... it feels familiar. I don't know why, maybe it's just what this staff is...is doing. Maybe it's...it's alerting me that we are in the right place."

And so Helicopter Jim took the staff and as he exited (HELICOPTER NAME), he stood right in front of this huge cliff, by this huge mountainside...

HJ: "Okay, like, where do I go from this point on?"

PRINCESS EVA: "Well, maybe...maybe there's a secret passage. Maybe you have to do something with the staff."

MR. CAPE: "Why don't we just walk around the area and just see if there's... if anything happens?"

And so Helicopter Jim, Scott, Zaiah, Princess Eva, Mr. Cape, and Mikhail exited (HELICOPTER NAME) and walked around a bit.

HJ: "Uh, I...I...I feel like this is the right area. I don't see where else we can go. But I, I...I do... I do sense that we need to go through this wall."

And so he took out January and held onto it, and he used it for wisdom, strength of the mind.

HJ: "Absolutely, we need to go through this wall."

SCOTT: "What do you mean *through* the wall? How are we going to go *through* the wall?"

HJ: "I'll just use August."

Sure enough, Helicopter Jim puts January back into his pouch, takes out August, becomes invisible, and walks right through the wall.

ZAIAH: "Whoa, he just went through the wall. Where… where are you? Jim, where are you?"

All of a sudden, a large portion of the side of the cliff opens up from the bottom to the top. This huge block of rock lifts up and opens up… big enough that they can see inside of this place. But not big enough for (HELICOPTER NAME) to go in. Everyone else is able to enter, so they walk in. And it is filled with blue crystals everywhere. The same crystals that are on the staff that Helicopter Jim is holding.

And as Helicopter Jim is holding the staff, the crystal on his staff becomes so bright that they can no longer look at it.

SCOTT: "Jim, what is happening that it's so bright?"

HJ: "I don't know. I can feel energy though, leaving the crystal. I sense it."

And all of a sudden, from the crystal that Helicopter Jim was holding, it fires off light in every direction and hits all of the other crystals in this area. And all of the crystals shatter, unveiling a massive wall on the other side of this huge separation between them and the wall. And Helicopter Jim looks around and they're in this huge cavern, this huge area with this separation between them and this huge wall.

And Helicopter Jim goes to the edge, looks down and all he sees is... it almost looks like blue molten lava. He can feel the heat, but it's blue.

HJ: "Come...come see this. What... look, what is this? That is definitely not lava, but it definitely has the same heat as lava."

MIKHAIL: "That's not lava. That's plasma."

HJ: "What do you mean plasma? What's...what is plasma?"

MIKHAIL: "Well, just to be... to...to make it sound easy, where we can understand, it's... it...it can do the same damage as regular lava. So, don't touch that. Just don't-don't fall in there."

HJ: "Okay, got it! Hey, look down there. What is... what is that area down there?"

SCOTT: "Where? What are you looking at?"

HJ: "Look over there. Don't... look...look toward the left. You see down there. There's that... there's that...that ridge there, look really good. There's a bridge."

SCOTT: "I...I'm not... we're not crossing that bridge! Are you crazy!? Look at how far down it is."

HJ: "Well, apparently that's where we should go."

PRINCESS EVA: "Uh, I...I agree. I agree Jim. I think that's where we need to go. There's no other area we can cross."

MR. CAPE: "Yeah, I think that's where we need to go. Otherwise, where else, uh… how else are we going to cross over?"

And so they started to make their way down to the bridge… (HELICOPTER NAME) stayed on the outside…

HELICOPTER: "I can't fit through the opening, so I'll stay right here. You guys can go ahead. I'll watch from afar."

HJ: "Okay, just...just, you know, um, be safe up there."

HELICOPTER: "Well, you be safe down there."

HJ: "We will."

So, Helicopter Jim and everyone else started to cross the bridge. And as they're crossing the bridge, something doesn't seem right.

AND THAT WILL BE THE NEXT ADVENTURE OF HELICOPTER JIM.

Adventure 130

On the last adventure of Helicopter Jim, the blue crystal staff guided Jim to where the Stone of June was located.

(HELICOPTER NAME) was able to use Jim's thoughts to guide them to where they needed to fly to. After some time, they found themselves in a barren land, which looked like a place devastated by earthquakes...yet it felt so familiar to Jim.

As they landed in the spot the staff guided them to, they were at the bottom of a massive cliff...with nothing else around them. Jim used wisdom from January and knew they needed to go through the wall of the cliff. So Jim used August to turn invisible...and walked through the wall. Jim was able to open a portion of the side of the cliff to let everyone in.

There was a large separation between where they stood and where they needed to go. They saw deep down below them, hot blue plasma with a bridge that they could cross over to the other side.

And so they started to make their way down to the bridge... (HELICOPTER NAME) stayed on the outside...

HELICOPTER: "I can't fit through the opening, so I'll stay right here. You guys can go ahead. I'll watch from afar."

HJ: "Okay, just...just, you know, um, be safe up there."

HELICOPTER: "Well, you be safe down there."

HJ: "We will."

So, Helicopter Jim and everyone else started to cross the bridge. And as they're crossing the bridge, something doesn't seem right.

AND NOW WE BEGIN THE ADVENTURES OF HELICOPTER JIM!

MIKHAIL: "Okay, I...I have that feeling again."

ZAIAH: "Same here. What is happening?"

Helicopter Jim noticed that the plasma was starting to rise, and they are halfway across the bridge.

HJ: "Okay, what… do we run all the way over to that side, or… what do we do?"

All of a sudden, the bridge starts to crumble.

HJ: "We've got to get off of this bridge!"

And so they're all trying to run back to where they came from. And as they're running, the bridge slowly breaks apart. Princess Eva, Mikhail, Mr. Cape and Scott make it to the other side. The bridge finally collapses. Helicopter Jim and Zaiah fall towards the plasma, but thankfully they landed on pieces of the bridge and they have no idea what to do. Zaiah is able to leap toward the other side to safety, where Mr. Cape and everybody else were.

Helicopter Jim is drifting further down, but he's drifting closer to the wall on the other side. He sees a small little area, where he can jump to and he jumps and he just makes it and grabs onto one of the rocks on the wall. Helicopter Jim is hanging on for his life. He takes out January and uses it for strength. And he's holding on to the rock, and the plasma is rising and Helicopter Jim has to now climb up this wall. And so he's climbing up the wall, and as he's climbing up the wall, he has to feel his way up.

And the wall begins to...it's not as solid as the area he jumped on. And now it's starting to turn almost to like clay and as he's reaching into different cracks and crevices of the wall to climb up, it slowly starts to crumble and he slides to the left and to the right and he's trying to grab on. Everybody is telling Jim to hang on tightly, and they don't know what to do.

Helicopter Jim is now slowly climbing up and the wall is cracking a little bit and as it's doing so, Helicopter Jim is wondering what he should do. And so as he's climbing on the wall, Mr. Cape notices something...

MR. CAPE: "Jim, the more you climb, and the more you're feeling into the cracks and crevices the more the wall is crumbling. It almost seems like this...this huge wall has...has... it has a pattern to it, where your hands are going. So feel for edges because that's... you can use those edges just...just remove the...the hardened clay and keep scraping it so that you can... you can find a ledge and...and where your hand can grab a hold of. Just keep doing what you're doing and...and...and you should be fine."

And Helicopter Jim is grabbing certain areas and the plasma continues to rise. Helicopter Jim is climbing all the way up and as he's climbing up, as he looks down, he sees the plasma continuing to rise and now it is almost so high that it's going to overflow to where everyone is as well as where (HELICOPTER NAME) is.

HELICOPTER: "Hurry...get in!"

Everybody runs up to (HELICOPTER NAME) and jumps in.

Jim is on the other side and he's looking down… he doesn't know what to do. So he rests his legs in the cracks so that he can take a break, just so that he can think… he has to think fast because the plasma is now rising up closer to him.

And as he's doing so, he remembers what the Darkhood leader said, that the staff will guide him to the Stone of June. So Helicopter Jim puts the Stone of January in its pouch and removes the staff from his holster and holds on to it. And as he's hanging on to the staff, he just trusts that it's going to lead him to June. As he's holding the staff, the staff begins to shake in his hand and he's hanging on tight to it.

He's hanging on tight, and he feels the staff pulling at him and is now pulling him off of the wall…

HJ: "Whoa, whoa, whoa...no, no, no...don't make me fall off of this ledge...what...what am I going to do? It's gonna pull me off of the wall and I'm gonna fall."

And it's pulling him and pulling him. Jim can't hang on anymore and he's losing strength, and as the staff is pulling him it pulls him off of the ledge and Jim begins to fall and he's heading toward the plasma and right before he hits the plasma…

AND THAT WILL BE THE NEXT ADVENTURE OF HELICOPTER JIM.

Adventure 131

On the last adventure of Helicopter Jim, as they were crossing the bridge, the plasma began to rise and at the same time, the bridge begins to crumble. Princess Eva, Mikhail, Mr. Cape and Scott make it to the other side. Helicopter Jim and Zaiah fall but land on small pieces of the bridge that fell into the plasma. Helicopter Jim drifts to the other side and climbs the wall. He digs his fingers and feet into areas of the wall that are soft enough to create crevices enough to hold himself up.

And as he's doing so, he remembers what the Darkhood leader said, that the staff will guide him to the Stone of June. So Helicopter Jim puts the Stone of January in its pouch and removes the staff from his holster and holds on to it. And as he's hanging on to the staff, he just trusts that it's going to lead him to June. As he's holding the staff, the staff begins to shake in his hand and he's hanging on tight to it.

He's hanging on tight, and he feels the staff pulling at him and is now pulling him off of the wall...

HJ: "Whoa, whoa, whoa...no, no, no...don't make me fall off of this ledge...what...what am I going to do? It's gonna pull me off of the wall and I'm gonna fall."

And it's pulling him and pulling him. Jim can't hang on anymore and he's losing strength, and as the staff is pulling him it pulls him off of the ledge and Jim begins to fall and he's heading toward the plasma and right before he hits the plasma...

AND NOW WE BEGIN THE ADVENTURES OF HELICOPTER JIM!

And right before Jim hits the plasma... all he hears is an arrow shoot right under him (SHHTOOK), and he lands on the arrow...and as he's trying to balance on the arrow, he turns around, and he sees Mr. Cape using the UnbreakaBow.

Mr. Cape shoots another arrow, Helicopter Jim can now step on the arrows and he shoots another arrow. Helicopter Jim can now move...

HJ: "Yesssss! Mr. Cape, good job. Keep shooting arrows, the staff is pulling me in that direction."

Helicopter Jim held out the staff and it kept pulling him alongside of the wall and Mr. Cape kept shooting arrows into the wall and because he has infinite arrows, he keeps shooting and Jim uses them to step up the wall. So as he's stepping on these arrows, Helicopter Jim is going higher and higher on this wall, and as he's heading up on this wall, he sees a small tiny little opening at the top and the staff, with the blue crystal, leads him right into that opening.

Helicopter Jim goes into the opening, crawls into it, and has to crawl through this opening for a little while, and it's tight in there but he has enough light from the blue crystal staff that he can see up ahead. And as he's going through this long, small tunnel that he has to crawl through, he sees up ahead this bright blue glow. As Helicopter Jim is going through this tunnel. He gets closer and closer to the end.

As he comes through the tunnel, he looks down over the edge of this opening and at the bottom he sees a bright blue glow. The staff is now shaking and Helicopter Jim doesn't know what to do because if he lets the staff pull him, it's going to pull him off of this ledge where he's on the other side now, where the bright blue glow is, and he's going to fall from a high height.

Helicopter Jim doesn't know what to do and he doesn't know how to get down but then he trusts that the staff will guide him. Helicopter Jim hangs on tightly to the staff and slowly crawls. And as the staff is pulling at him, it's pulling even stronger. Helicopter Jim hangs on to the staff and the staff is pulling toward that glow which is way down at the bottom. Helicopter Jim just trusts... and he crawls out of that opening on that other side and he begins to fall.

But he hangs on tightly to the staff and closes his eyes as he's falling...

HJ: (SPEAK QUICKLY AND NERVOUSLY) "Please don't hit the ground. Please don't hit the ground. Please don't hit the ground. I don't wanna die. I don't wanna die. I don't wanna die."

And as he's closing his eyes, he's feeling himself falling and falling and falling and then all of a sudden, he doesn't feel like he's falling anymore.

Jim slowly opens his eyes and looks around and it's hard for him to see because all he sees is a bright blue light all around him and he's having a hard time seeing.

(SQUINT YOUR EYES, AND USE YOUR HANDS TO SHIELD) He's squinting his eyes and puts his hand in front of his eyes while he's holding the staff with the blue crystal so he can see.. Just then, the blue crystal shoots out a light directly at the center of this glow and the blue crystal on the staff begins to shake. Helicopter Jim is trying to see in front of him, squinting his eyes... and then all of a sudden... the blue crystal explodes

(EXPLOSION SOUND F/X)... he looks and he can vaguely see something right in front of him,

And as Jim is looking right in front of him, the glow slowly starts to dim. And as Helicopter Jim adjusts his eyes, right in front of him... is... the Stone of June! Helicopter Jim reaches out his hand, takes a hold of June and holds it up.

And now Jim has within his possession, the Stone of June! But what he's now thinking of is, how does he get out of this place because the entrance is so high that he can't even get to it. The staff no longer is able to help him. Helicopter Jim is stuck and doesn't know what to do. But far in the corner, he sees a large stone and it looks like it's covering another entrance or an exit. Helicopter Jim goes over to the stone and tries to move the stone, but he's not able to. So he takes out January. January gives him the strength he needs to push the stone on the side.

So Helicopter Jim pushes the stone on the side and as he does, there is another passage. He uses January to light up the place and he can see that there is a way to walk and an area for him to walk through. And so Helicopter Jim goes through that area and he's walking through it and he's going in a direction that seems like he's going higher and higher. He's walking upwards and he's going around a bend in this passageway. And as he's turning, he feels that it's getting steeper and steeper and he's climbing uphill in this passageway.

And as he's coming up through the passageway, he sees...

AND THAT WILL BE THE NEXT ADVENTURE OF HELICOPTER JIM.

Adventure 132

On the last adventure of Helicopter Jim, Jim cannot hold onto the wall any longer. What doesn't help is that the blue crystal staff pulls Jim off of the wall, causing him to fall toward the hot plasma down below. Thankfully, Mr. Cape uses the UnbreakaBow to shoot arrows for Jim to use to climb to safety.

Helicopter Jim follows the pull of the staff and is able to retrieve the Stone of June on the other side of the wall. Jim is in an area where it looks like there is no exit, but far in the corner, he sees a large stone and it looks like it's covering another entrance or an exit.

So Helicopter Jim uses January for strength and pushes the stone on the side and as he does, there is another passage and he uses January to light up the place and he can see that there is a way to walk and an area for him to walk through. And so Helicopter Jim goes through that area and he's walking through it and he's going in a direction that seems like he's going higher and higher. He's walking upwards and he's going around a bend in this passageway. And as he's turning, he feels that it's getting steeper and steeper and he's climbing uphill in this passageway.

And as he's coming up through the passageway, he sees...

AND NOW WE BEGIN THE ADVENTURES OF HELICOPTER JIM!

And as he's coming up through the passageway, he sees... light up ahead which means that he's now going to exit from where he is. And as he exits, he finds himself outside where (HELICOPTER NAME) is.

HJ: "Hey guys! Look… How...how did I get on this side?"

HELICOPTER: "Where did you come from?"

PRINCESS EVA: "How did you get out here? What... how… Where did you come from?"

HJ: "I came right through that tiny opening right there. Why didn't we see that when we first came here?"

HELICOPTER: "Because that opening wasn't there when we first came here. Look at the video footage that I have. You can see here there is no opening. That opening only appeared when you came through...riiiiight, there. That was amazing."

SCOTT: "What? How did you get there? What did you do?"

And Helicopter Jim pulled out June from his pouch…

HJ: "I retrieved… (SAY WITH EXCITEMENT WHILE NODDING YOUR HEAD) the Stone of June!"

Everyone was celebrating and excited that Jim retrieved June...

MR. CAPE: "Yes! Well done, Jim. Well done!"

MIKHAIL: "Jim, way to go. Was it difficult? Did you have to do something difficult? Was it dangerous?"

HJ: "Well, it wasn't really dangerous Mikhail. It was just different. You know, each stone I guess is different, but I...I...I think right now, we need to… we need to find a way for us to be able to..."

And as Jim was talking, he looked at the other side where he was climbing the wall where he had to scale the wall when the plasma was rising and he noticed that there was a shape on the wall where he was climbing... where his hands were removing a lot of the dirt and he looked at it and he could see a shape in it.

HJ: "Hey, guys, take a look at the wall where I was climbing. Take a look at it."

ZAIAH: "That looks pretty interesting."

PRINCESS EVA: "What do you mean pretty interesting? What... I don't... I don't see what you guys see."

ZAIAH: "Mikhail, do you see that?"

MIKHAIL: "Yes, I do."

SCOTT: "I don't get it. What are you guys looking at?"

HJ: "Don't you see where I was... where my hands were gripping and where my feet were? And look at that area right there."

SCOTT: "I have no idea what you're talking about. All I see, are the areas where you were putting your hands and where you were removing dirt... and where your feet were. Well, I don't... I don't get what you're looking at."

HJ: "Do you see right there...that area where my hands were... and my feet? Do you see where I removed the dir... the dirt?"

SCOTT "Yes."

HJ: "What does that look like to you?"

PRINCESS EVA: "That looks like the head, the top part of an... of some kind of bird."

SCOTT: (FRUSTRATED TONE) "What? What? It

doesn't... it looks nothing like a bird. What do you mean a bird? That looks nothing like a bird."

AND THAT WILL BE THE NEXT ADVENTURE OF HELICOPTER JIM.

Adventure 133

On the last adventure of Helicopter Jim, Jim was able to celebrate with everyone that he retrieved the Stone of June.

As they were celebrating, Jim noticed that there was a shape on the wall caused by Jim trying to find areas to hold onto in the areas where the dirt was soft.

Everyone could see a shape...except for Scott...

SCOTT: "I have no idea what you're talking about. All I see are the areas where you were putting your hands and where you were removing dirt... and where your feet were. Well, I don't... I don't get what you're looking at."

HJ: "Do you see right there...that area where my hands were... and my feet? Do you see where I removed the dir... the dirt?"

SCOTT "Yes."

HJ: "What does that look like to you?"

PRINCESS EVA: "That looks like the head, the top part of an... of some kind of bird."

SCOTT: (FRUSTRATED TONE) "What? What? It doesn't... it looks nothing like a bird. What do you mean a bird? That looks nothing like a bird."

AND NOW WE BEGIN THE ADVENTURES OF HELICOPTER JIM!

MIKHAIL: "Scott, not the kind of birds you know of. Now, imagine not just a bird, but a large bird."

SCOTT: "A large bird? What am I even looking for? All I see is where...Ohhhhhhhh, now, I see. Wow, that thing is huge! If... tha...that shape right there? Tha...that's just the...the...the head, the top and the... Okay, I see right there. And that's the beak. I...there's the beak where it curves and then the top... Whoa, I see that. Okay, okay. Now, I see it. Okay. Fine. What...what does that mean?"

HJ: "Maybe...maybe it's letting us know that Blue is somewhere around here. Hey, (HELICOPTER NAME), are you able to scan the wall or...or...or maybe do some type of, uh, scan with the Trxsol and maybe there's something you can find?"

HELICOPTER: "Absolutely. Let me do a quick scan and let me do some scanning that will be able to see what's behind it as well as do some type of topography for it."

And so as (HELICOPTER NAME) scanned the wall, they're all looking at the video screen of the image that comes through and they can see a large shape...which looks like an eagle..

HJ: "See, I told you. Look at that. That's...that's...that's... that has to be, uh, uh, some type of...of clue or some type of evidence that Blue is somewhere around here."

SCOTT: "What do we do then? How... where do... where do we go? I mean, where else is there to go? The...the staff brought us here. So w-w-where do we go from here?"

HJ: "I have no idea."

HELICOPTER: "Jim, I hate to tell you this, but I sense that Fury is nearby."

HJ: "So what do we do? What... I mean if Fury comes here

and we don't have Blue... we don't have a chance. How...how do we... how do we fight off Fury?"

SCOTT: "Well, we do have new gear and armor. Maybe we could try that. We have (HELICOPTER NAME). I mean what...what...what else can we do?"

HJ: "Well, I don't... I don't know what to do."

And so he took out January for wisdom and wisdom said, "Stay here."

HJ: "We...we gotta stay here. Blue must be around here somewhere. (THINKING DEEPLY) Maybe we need to... let's-let's-let's-let's figure out how we can do this. And maybe what we can do is somehow figure out why that wall has that carving of Blue."

Just then Scott remembered something.

SCOTT: "Hey Jim, remember what the 12 Pillars said? Well, the Pillar of June, remember that was the only one that had an inscription on it? "Life is in the eye."

HJ: "That's right. But what does that mean?"

PRINCESS: "Maybe...maybe the life of Blue is in its eye."

HJ: "Okay, but what does that do for me? I mean, what... I don't even know what to do with that. What do I... what do I do? 'The life is in the eye.' I don't even know where Blue is so how would I know that there's life in it? I... I don't... I don't... I don't get it. I don't...I don't know how that helps. Maybe that's just for me to know when I do find Blue that, 'The life is in the eye.' I don't know."

MIKHAIL: "Jim, it could possibly be that the only way Blue comes to life is if you climb up that wall and put the stone into the area where his eye would be."

HJ: "Well, how do I get to the other side? There's still all of that plasma. I can't get there."

MR. CAPE: "I have an idea. Princess, give me the chain."

And so Mr. Cape attached the chain to the Infinite Arrow...

MR. CAPE: "Jim, I am going to shoot this arrow across with the chain and connect it to (HELICOPTER NAME) and you're going to have to use the chain to cross over the plasma."

AND THAT WILL BE THE NEXT ADVENTURE OF HELICOPTER JIM.

Adventure 134

On the last adventure of Helicopter Jim, Mikhail, Jim, Mr. Cape, Scott, Princess Eva and Zaiah were trying to figure out what the carving of the shape of an eagle meant, on the wall. Mikhail comes up with an idea...

MIKHAIL: "Jim, it could possibly be that the only way Blue comes to life is if you climb up that wall and put the stone into the area where his eye would be."

HJ: "Well, how do I get to the other side? There's still all of that plasma. I can't get there."

MR. CAPE: "I have an idea. Princess, give me the chain."

And so Mr. Cape attached the chain to the Infinite Arrow...

MR. CAPE: "Jim, I am going to shoot this arrow across with the chain and connect it to (HELICOPTER NAME) and you're going to have to use the chain to cross over the plasma."

AND NOW WE BEGIN THE ADVENTURES OF HELICOPTER JIM!

HJ: "What!? There's no way I'm going to be able to cross over that. You know how hot that is? I'm going to have to cross... no way! There's no way I can do that. You... and if you shoot it high, you know how hard it is for me to climb up? I'm going to have to like, shimmy up the...the...the chain. That's not going to be easy. And I can't hold January in my hand to use strength.

SCOTT: "Well, now's a good time to field test the Final Cloak."

HJ: "That's the worst idea ever Scott. I'm not going to field test the Final Cloak over hot plasma."

SCOTT: "You don't need to go over the hot plasma to test it. Why don't you just put it on now and then go near the plasma and see...see what it does?"

HJ: "Oh, okay, I'll try your idea."

So Helicopter Jim put on The Final Cloak and he disappeared. As he walked closer to the plasma, he did feel protected. There was still heat, but not as much. And so he came back to Scott...

HJ: "Scott, you were right. I...I can't... it... there's still some heat, but it's not as bad. Hey, let's try that Mr. Cape."

So Mr. Cape shot the arrow across and it got lodged into the wall. Helicopter Jim then was able to climb across using Final Cloak as his protection and as he's going across, he's getting tired because his arms are becoming fatigued, more and more tired. And his arms are drained of energy. And he's almost to the other side.

HJ: (USE STRAINING VOICE) "I can't hold on. It's too hard... my hands are tired!"

PRINCESS EVA: "You got this Jim. You can do this. Just keep going little by little. Are you almost there?"

SCOTT: "Yeah Jim, you can do it. You...you only have a couple more feet, I can see where you are... I see the chain dipping where you are... you can do this."

Helicopter Jim was struggling and trying to do his very best and he's hanging on as best as possible. Jim is almost there... so he swings his body back and forth to gain some momentum...then at the perfect time, he swings toward the other side and lets go of the chain... and lands on this one tiny ledge and holds himself there. And he grabs onto a section and he can barely hang on because his arms are weak and his hands have no strength left. And he's holding on.

Jim is trying to make sure he doesn't fall into the plasma. So he's trying to find any crack or crevice where he can put his hands. And as he's doing so, he keeps removing dirt and he keeps carving into the wall, places where his hand can hold on to and his feet can find some type of footing and grip. And as he's doing so, Mikhail notices that Helicopter Jim is actually carving out a shape that looks like the head of a large eagle.

MR. CAPE: "Hey, Jim, keep carving. We can see a shape being formed from all the areas that you're digging into."

HJ: "Yeah, there are some areas that the...the dirt on the wall is soft, like I can... I can actually carve out of the wall, these certain areas."

PRINCESS EVA: "Hey, Jim, why don't you go to the left. Keep going to the left."

HJ: "To the left, uh, that's hard. I can't reach anymore with my feet. It's too... it's too far of a distance. There's nothing to carve."

SCOTT: "Well, stretch out as much as you can."

ZAIAH: "Jim, there's an area where you can hold on to. It's...it's below your left leg, if you can... if you can find a soft spot where you can carve out some dirt. See if you can do that, see if your foot can go in that area."

So, Helicopter Jim keeps trying to carve out of the wall, soft dirt so that at least his feet can find some type of crack where he can rest and at least regain some strength.

MR. CAPE: "Remember, Jim, that the Stone of June is able to bring Blue to life. And if, 'The life is in the eye,' then maybe you have to find the eye of this carving, and maybe that might do something."

HJ: "Well, if I can... I can't even see what you guys are seeing. If I can find the eye, that would be great."

PRINCESS EVA: "That's what I'm saying Jim. If you go to the left, maybe... even where your foot is, if you can find an area that might be soft, I think that's an area where that might be where the eye would be. You just have to stretch a little bit."

Helicopter Jim is trying his best and he's stretching and he's pushing his foot against the wall, trying to find any area that would be soft, any soft dirt, where his foot can go into it. And, finally, he feels some give of the wall. A little bit of the wall slowly begins to crumble away as he uses his left foot to scrape away dirt and he keeps pushing at it.

SCOTT: "There it is Jim! There it is! Perfect! Keep doing that. You see, your foot can fit in there. Perfect...perfect...perfect. Just keep doing that."

AND THAT WILL BE THE NEXT ADVENTURE OF HELICOPTER JIM.

Adventure 135

On the last adventure of Helicopter Jim, Mr. Cape shoots an arrow across to the other side, with the chain from Princess Eva attached to it and connects it to (HELICOPTER NAME) so that Jim can make his way to the other side.

Jim uses The Final Cloak for protection and gets to the other side safely. He then climbs the wall and begins to carve away some of the dirt in specific areas as Princess Eva, Mr. Cape, Scott and Zaiah are guiding him...

MR. CAPE: "Remember, Jim, that the Stone of June is able to bring Blue to life. And if, 'The life is in the eye,' then maybe you have to find the eye of this carving, and maybe that might do something."

HJ: "Well, if I can... I can't even see what you guys are seeing. If I can find the eye, that would be great."

PRINCESS EVA: "That's what I'm saying Jim. If you go to the left, maybe... even where your foot is, if you can find an area that might be soft, I think that's an area where that might be where the eye would be. You just have to stretch a little bit."

Helicopter Jim is trying his best and he's stretching and he's pushing his foot against the wall, trying to find any area that would be soft, any soft dirt, where his foot can go into it. And, finally, he feels some give of the wall. A little bit of the wall slowly begins to crumble away as he uses his left foot to scrape away dirt and he keeps pushing at it.

SCOTT: "There it is Jim! There it is! Perfect! Keep doing that. You see, your foot can fit in there. Perfect...perfect...perfect.

Just keep doing that."

AND NOW WE BEGIN THE ADVENTURES OF HELICOPTER JIM!

HJ: (STRAINING VOICE) "I can't... hold on... I...I...I...I got it. At least I can rest now."

PRINCESS EVA: "No, don't rest. That's... uh, we can see now the...the...the... the shape of the top part of the eagle's head, we can see it! And right where your foot is, that's exactly where the eye would be."

HJ: "Okay, but if 'The life is in the eye,' I don't... then what do I do if 'The life is in the eye?' I don't know what to do. I mean, if...if June is able to bring Blue to life, I have... I have June. I...I don't know what to do with it."

MIKHAIL: "Hey, Jim, how big is that hole where your foot is?"

HJ: "What do you mean how big is it? It's just a... it's just a...a...a small portion. I mean, I can't dig any more around it."

MIKHAIL: "So. Can you... can you keep going? I mean, is it... can it get bigger than that?"

HJ: "No, it can't. It's probably the same size as... (WIDE EYED) the Stone."

So Jim took out the Stone of June and he looked at the Stone of June and tried to look at where his foot was, but he really couldn't see the hole because his foot is in it..

HJ: "Hey Mikhail, can you see the size of the Stone and the hole where my foot is? It looks the same size, doesn't it?"

MIKHAIL: "Yeah, that's...that's what we're thinking. We were thinking that maybe the Stone is supposed to go there. Because if 'The life is in the eye,' and the Stone brings Blue to life, see what happens when you put the Stone of June in the eye of the carving."

HJ: "I'll try. I can't... I can't reach though. I can't... I can't... if I... if I go any further, I'm going to fall and I can barely hang on with my hand, with my right hand. And I can't... I can't stretch far enough to get it."

MR. CAPE: "You know what I'll do, Jim, I'm going to shoot another arrow, and I need you to hang on to the arrow where I shoot it, and then I'm going to shoot another arrow for your footing. That way you can stand on the arrows, and then you'll be able to put the Stone in. But because the arrows dissolve, you're gonna have to do it quickly and then hang on tightly to another arrow. I'll just keep shooting arrows and you just get to keep hanging on and...and from one arrow to the next."

HJ: "Okay, I can do that. But you...you... make sure you keep those arrows coming and...and I'll do my best."

So, Mr. Cape shot a couple of arrows where Helicopter Jim could hang on to them. And as he did, he took the Stone of June and placed it in the hole and it fit perfectly. And right when Helicopter Jim did that, all of a sudden, the whole entire wall broke, just exploded. And out of the wall comes this huge, giant eagle. It was Blue, the giant eagle! And because the wall exploded, Helicopter Jim went flying into the air, and now he's coming down. And all he hears is a loud screech from Blue, (EAGLE SOUND).

And now Helicopter Jim is falling toward the liquid plasma and they don't know what to do. And Helicopter Jim is trying to use The Final Cloak but he can't... he can't cover himself fully and he's heading toward the liquid plasma.

PRINCESS EVA: "Jim, no!"

Jim is falling towards the plasma. He's at twenty feet, fifteen feet, ten...and right before Jim hits the liquid plasma, right above him...

AND THAT WILL BE THE NEXT ADVENTURE OF HELICOPTER JIM.

Adventure 136

On the last adventure of Helicopter Jim, Jim was able to locate the area where the Stone of June could be put. Jim was trying his best to hold on to the wall, but he was losing his grip.

So, Mr. Cape shot a couple of arrows where Helicopter Jim could hang on to them. And as he did, he took the Stone of June and placed it in the hole and it fit perfectly. And right when Helicopter Jim did that, all of a sudden, the whole entire wall broke, just exploded. And out of the wall comes this huge, giant eagle. It was Blue, the giant eagle! And because the wall exploded, Helicopter Jim went flying into the air, and now he's coming down. And all he hears is a loud screech from Blue, (EAGLE SOUND).

And now Helicopter Jim is falling toward the liquid plasma and they don't know what to do. And Helicopter Jim is trying to use The Final Cloak but he can't... he can't cover himself fully and he's heading toward the liquid plasma.

PRINCESS EVA: "Jim, no!"

Jim is falling towards the plasma. He's at twenty feet, fifteen feet, ten...and right before Jim hits the liquid plasma, right above him...

AND NOW WE BEGIN THE ADVENTURES OF HELICOPTER JIM!

Right above him... comes Blue and scoops him up, he catches him. Helicopter Jim is being carried by Blue. And Blue flies around in that area, exits the mountain and heads into the sky and he flies all the way up into the sky and tosses Jim onto its back.

Jim is hanging on for dear life…

HJ: (SCARED AND SPEAK FAST) "Oh my goodness. Oh my goodness. Oh my goodness. Oh my goodness."

And he doesn't know what to do. He's just hanging on. Blue is huge and Jim is amazed at just how big Blue is…

HJ: "Okay, okay, I…I get it. You're free but we don't have to be this high. Can we go back now?"

And Blue turns around, swoops back, swoops back down and goes back to where everyone else is and Blue is coming in fast…

SCOTT: "Wow, did you see-see that? That is incredible." And Mikhail, Princess Eva, Mr. Cape, and Zaiah are all amazed at what just happened.

Princess Eva is cheering and jumping for joy…

PRINCESS EVA: "Woohoo, look at that! That is amazing and Blue is massive."

SCOTT: "Yeah, he's…he's bigger than my house! We can all fit on him, my goodness! When…when…when it said 'Blue the Giant Eagle,' I thought like, a giant eagle not like a giant, giant of an eagle. That's amazing. Well, here they come!"

And Blue lands right where (HELICOPTER NAME) is and they all come running outside to see what's happening and how Jim is doing and Blue lands and puts his wing down so Helicopter Jim can exit off of his back.

Jim climbs off of Blue's wing and lands on the ground and he is thankful that he made it back to land.

HJ: "Did you guys see that? This is incredible. Look at how big Blue is."

And Blue looks at Jim and stares at him for a little while...

MIKHAIL: "Jim, Blue is... he's focusing on you because he knows you're the Chosen One and he wants you to know that he's here for you. That he...he will do his best to protect you and help you on your journey...and also, that's funny Blue...(LIGHT CHUCKLE)."

SCOTT: "What's so funny?"

MIKHAIL: "Blue...Blue is wondering why you look so young Jim. He didn't think that the Chosen One would be a kid. (CHUCKLE)"

HJ: "Oh, that's... ha ha ha, very funny, Blue. You didn't know I was gonna be a kid. I didn't know you were gonna be like the size of a building but you're...you're you can move pretty quick for being such a huge eagle."

So Helicopter Jim, Mr. Cape, Mikhail, Scott, Princess Eva, and Zaiah needed to find a way out of that area because Fury was on his way...

HJ: "(HELICOPTER NAME) do you have any coordinates to where Fury is?"

HELICOPTER: "He's still on his way. He's still a far distance off but he's coming quickly."

MIKHAIL: "Hey, Blue...do you know of Fury? Do you know who Fury is and what Fury is capable of doing?"

And Blue was able to communicate with Mikhail...

MIKHAIL: Guys, Blue knows exactly who Fury is and what needs to be done. Fury will not stop at anything until the Chosen One is destroyed. We must also remember that just as much as Fury is out to destroy Jim, Blue is just as dedicated to do anything necessary to protect you, Jim."

HJ: "That's...that's a relief. I mean, I'm thankful Blue. I'm thankful but I...I'd rather... I'd rather us figure out how to do this together. That way, together, we can all be safe."

And Blue let out a loud screech once again in agreement (EAGLE SCREECH).

HJ: "Okay guys, I know Fury is on his way, but we still have a lot of work to do. We need to find the other Stones, and right now. Because of what we just experienced with Blue, we have the opportunity to continue on and look for the Stone of September. It's here on Diamond Crust and we...we...we can... we can find it."

And Blue speaks to Mikhail...

MIKHAIL: "Jim, Blue knows the area where September may be."

HJ: "That's great! Let's go there. Even if Blue doesn't know exactly where it is, at least we know the area or at least it'll be in that area."

And so everyone got into (HELICOPTER NAME). And as Jim was about to climb into the Helicopter, he turned around and looked at Blue...

HJ: "Hey, Blue, can I jump on again?"

And Blue let out a loud screech (EAGLE SCREECH).

MIKHAIL: "Yeah, that was a yes. Go ahead, jump on."

SCOTT: "Hey, wa...wait, is it... can I... can I jump on too? Is that okay?"

And Blue looked at Scott and just stared at him for a little while…

AND THAT WILL BE THE NEXT ADVENTURE OF HELICOPTER JIM.

Adventure 137

On the last adventure of Helicopter Jim, Mr. Cape, Mikhail, Scott, Princess Eva, Zaiah, and Jim, were able to bring Blue the Giant Eagle to life. Mikhail is also able to communicate with Blue.

MIKHAIL: "Jim, Blue knows the area where September may be."

HJ: "That's great! Let's go there. Even if Blue doesn't know exactly where it is, at least we know the area or at least it'll be in that area."

And so everyone got into (HELICOPTER NAME). And as Jim was about to climb into the Helicopter, he turned around and looked at Blue...

HJ: "Hey, Blue, can I jump on again?"

And Blue let out a loud screech (EAGLE SCREECH).

MIKHAIL: "Yeah, that was a yes. Go ahead, jump on."

SCOTT: "Hey, wa...wait, is it... can I... can I jump on too? Is that okay?"

And Blue looked at Scott and just stared at him for a little while...

AND NOW WE BEGIN THE ADVENTURES OF HELICOPTER JIM!

MIKHAIL: "He's okay Scott. You can go on. He's just giving you a hard time."

And so Blue let down his wing. Jim and Scott were able to

climb on...

HJ: "Mikhail, you should come too, so you can help communicate with Blue..."

MIKHAIL: "Sounds good to me."

HJ: "Anybody else wanna come?"

MR. CAPE: "No thank you...I'm okay in (HELICOPTER NAME).

ZAIAH: "I'm with Mr. Cape."

HJ: "Princess, do you wanna... do you wanna come up, do you wanna fly?"

PRINCESS EVA: "I really don't want to. I mean, I'm not okay with... I'm okay with being in (HELICOPTER NAME) and flying but now you're talking about out in the open."

SCOTT: "Don't be scared. Come on, don't be scared."

PRINCESS EVA: "I'm not scared. I just don't..."

HJ: "What...what is... what...what's the matter?"

PRINCESS EVA: "Okay, I just don't like it when my hair gets very very messy. It looks... it gets poofy, okay!" (ROLLS HER EYES AND SIGHS)

HJ: "Oh my goodness, just get on. You can... you can always tie your hair up, do something with it, you'll be fine."

And so Princess Eva jumps on the wing of Blue and as she did, Scott looked at her and laughed under his breath...

SCOTT: (SLIGHT CHUCKLE) "Your hair, I can't believe out of everything that...that you're... you're able to do... you're fearless, you're a warrior princess. Out of everything... your weakness is...your hair!?"

PRINCESS EVA: "Yeah, you're very funny Scott. Ha ha ha, yes, it's my hair, okay. Everyone has a weakness."

And as she passed by Scott, she flicked him on the back of his neck...

SCOTT: "Ow, ow, ow, what did you do that for?"

PRINCESS EVA: "See, that's your weakness."

SCOTT: "What...what is my weakness?"

HJ: "Wow Princess, that was...that was brutal. That was wow, Eva, you had to go there."

SCOTT: (SARCASTICALLY) "But it's not true, it's...it's not true, I know you're just joking because that...that's not true. Uh huh, very funny. Let's just go Jim, can we just go."

HJ: "Okay, let's go. Hey, Blue, take us to where you believe the Stone of September is located. Let's go."

And so Blue takes off with...with one push of its wings, one flap of his wings, they take off in an instant and (HELICOPTER NAME) follows behind while Jim, Princess Eva, and Scott are soaring through the air...

HJ: "Woohoo!"

They are flying very fast. (HELICOPTER NAME) is right behind them and as they're flying through the air, Helicopter Jim can see the entire land of Diamond Crust below them.

SCOTT: (FLYING ON BLUE, SPEAK WITH A RAISED VOICE) "This is amazing. Look at this entire area. What is...

what is that area over there?"

PRINCESS EVA: (FLYING ON BLUE, SPEAK WITH A RAISED VOICE) "I think that's... I think that area is...is the outlands and I...I don't...I don't remember ever going there."

SCOTT: (FLYING ON BLUE, SPEAK WITH A RAISED VOICE) "Ooh, look at that area! What is that area?"

PRINCESS EVA: (FLYING ON BLUE, SPEAK WITH A RAISED VOICE) "Oh that's... that's the... that's the...the...the Sanctuary Forest and we use that area for different things. We have various trees that grow there, we have forest friends there. So there are a lot of areas where the Stone could be, but it looks like Blue is going somewhere else. I don't know where he's gonna take us."

And as they're flying, Jim notices way off in the distance, a storm coming...

HJ: (FLYING ON BLUE, SPEAK WITH A RAISED VOICE) "Hey Blue, there's... I know you see that storm up ahead, uh, can we avoid that? Where...where are we heading to anyway?"

MIKHAIL: (FLYING ON BLUE, SPEAK WITH A RAISED VOICE) "Jim, you're not going to like this, but..."

SCOTT: (FLYING ON BLUE, SPEAK WITH A RAISED VOICE) "Well, judging by that look Blue just gave you Jim, I think that's where we're going."

MIKHAIL: (FLYING ON BLUE, SPEAK WITH A RAISED VOICE) "You guessed correctly Scott...according to Blue, that's exactly where we're going."

And as they head into the storm, they see lightning and rain and as they're getting closer, it gets darker and darker…

AND THAT WILL BE THE NEXT ADVENTURE OF HELICOPTER JIM.

Adventure 138

On the last adventure of Helicopter Jim, they were on their way in search of the Stone of September. Jim, Mikhail, Scott, and Princess Eva are riding on Blue.

And as they're flying, Jim notices way off in the distance, a storm coming...

HJ: (FLYING ON BLUE, SPEAK WITH A RAISED VOICE) "Hey Blue, there's... I know you see that storm up ahead, uh, can we avoid that? Where...where are we heading to anyway?"

MIKHAIL: (FLYING ON BLUE, SPEAK WITH A RAISED VOICE) "Jim, you're not going to like this, but..."

SCOTT: (FLYING ON BLUE, SPEAK WITH A RAISED VOICE) "Well, judging by that look Blue just gave you Jim, I think that's where we're going."

MIKHAIL: (FLYING ON BLUE, SPEAK WITH A RAISED VOICE) "You guessed correctly Scott...according to Blue, that's exactly where we're going."

And as they head into the storm, they see lightning and rain and as they're getting closer, it gets darker and darker...

AND NOW WE BEGIN THE ADVENTURES OF HELICOPTER JIM!

HJ: (FLYING ON BLUE, SPEAK WITH A RAISED VOICE) "Hey Scott, you know, as we get closer, we should... we should get into (HELICOPTER NAME) because it's going to, you know, it's going to be raining and...and...and now we're on the outside where the lightning can get us. So how about we get back into (HELICOPTER NAME)? What do you think Princess?"

PRINCESS EVA: (FLYING ON BLUE, SPEAK WITH A RAISED VOICE) "I agree, I think that's a smart idea."

HJ: (FLYING ON BLUE, SPEAK WITH A RAISED VOICE) "Hey (HELICOPTER NAME), we're going to have to board you because you see that lightning storm up ahead, we don't wanna be in that."

HELICOPTER: "Yeah, I got you."

(HELICOPTER NAME) comes close to Blue and Blue glides, opens his wings, and Helicopter Jim, Princess Eva, and Scott are able to walk to (HELICOPTER NAME) on Blue's wing.

And so one by one, they start walking on the wing of Blue and so Scott and Helicopter Jim allows Princess Eva to go first and so she runs across the wing of Blue and enters into (HELICOPTER NAME).

HJ: (FLYING ON BLUE, SPEAK WITH A RAISED VOICE) "Come on Scott, let's go. You and I can go, let's go."

And so they're both running on the wing of Blue and as they're getting closer to (HELICOPTER NAME), all of a sudden, this fireball hits Blue...(EAGLE SCREECH)

Scott barely makes it into the helicopter and Jim gets thrown from the wing of Blue and is now falling...

MR. CAPE: "Jim!"

They can see Jim falling in the sky and they turn around to see where this fireball came from... and they see Fury right behind them. Fury shoots off another fireball at Blue. Blue is able to dodge the fireball and turns toward Fury and Blue shoots off his own specialty... a ball of hardened ice. Blue shoots right at Fury's chest and hits Fury so hard that Fury is now flying out of control and tries to regain his ability to fly straight. Just then, Blue turns around and heads toward Jim because Jim is quickly falling... Jim is almost near the ground and Blue is flying as fast as he can... Jim is about to hit the ground when all of a sudden, Blue catches Jim with his claws and is able to bring Jim safely to land.

Lightning, thunder and rain is coming down at them and (HELICOPTER NAME) lands next to Jim. Mr. Cape exits (HELICOPTER NAME)...

MR. CAPE: "Jim, are you okay?"

HJ: "Yeah, I'm fine, I'm fine, I'm...I'm fine. That was just crazy! I... seriously, I mean, that was probably the scariest I've ever been... but Blue is so fast and, Fury, how...how could we not sense Fury coming? (HELICOPTER NAME), did you... did you not sense Fury?"

HELICOPTER: "I had no idea that Fury was here. I could not detect him, he got here so fast."

And so Helicopter Jim and the rest of the team are watching Fury and Blue battle in the sky. Fury regains his composure and shoots off another fireball at Blue. Blue dodges the fireball, sends off another ball of ice toward Fury and Fury is able to dodge the ball of ice. Fury once again attacks Blue, but not with a ball of fire this time.

He comes straight toward Blue. Blue heads straight towards Fury...

HJ: "We gotta do something, how can we help them? What can we do?"

HELICOPTER: "Jump in. Let's go, let's get up there."

And so Jim jumps into (HELICOPTER NAME) and Jim takes control...

HJ: "Okay, we gotta figure this out. We know that Fury is out to get me. That's his... that's his only goal. So we have to somehow cripple him, destroy him... something! We have to end him. I don't know what we're gonna do because he's...he's...he's made out of fire and he's so strong."

And Blue sends off a loud shriek (EAGLE SHRIEK SOUND) which shoots off tiny little pellets of water, and as it hits Fury, Fury lets off a scream (SHRIEK SOUND) because it's the water that Blue shoots at him that causes him to take on damage. And so as they're doing battle, Jim tells everyone to get equipped.

Jim grabs The Final Cloak and his Legendary Sword...

HJ: "Scott, grab your InvisiBow and The Final Cloak. Mikhail, grab your Power Sword and equip yourself with the Liquid Metal. Mr. Cape, bring your UnbreakaBow. Zaiah, bring your Power Sword and The Shield of Absorption. And Princess Eva... we're gonna need that chain."

PRINCESS EVA: "Zaiah?"

ZAIAH: "Yes Princess..."

PRINCESS EVA: "Give me Destiny…"

SCOTT: "That's the name of your sword? That… is cool."

And so they're all equipped.

HJ: "Okay, we're gonna have to do this together. (HELICOPTER NAME), take us up."

AND THAT WILL BE THE NEXT ADVENTURE OF HELICOPTER JIM.

Adventure 139

On the last adventure of Helicopter Jim, as they are on their way in search of September, they see a terrible storm ahead, so Jim, Scott, Mikhail, and Princess Eva need to get into (HELICOPTER NAME). Princess Eva, Mikhail, and Scott make it into the helicopter, but Jim is thrown from the wing of Blue because Fury showed up and shot off a fireball at Blue.

As Jim is falling, Blue is able to catch him and bring him to safety on land. Blue and Fury are in a battle, and Jim puts together a plan to help Blue.

Jim grabs The Final Cloak and his Legendary Sword…

HJ: "Scott, grab your InvisiBow and The Final Cloak. Mikhail, grab your Power Sword and equip yourself with the Liquid Metal. Mr. Cape, bring your UnbreakaBow. Zaiah, bring your Power Sword and The Shield of Absorption. And Princess Eva… we're gonna need that chain."

PRINCESS EVA: "Zaiah?"

ZAIAH: "Yes Princess…"

PRINCESS EVA: "Give me Destiny…"

SCOTT: "That's the name of your sword? That… is cool."

And so they're all equipped.

HJ: "Okay, we're gonna have to do this together. (HELICOPTER NAME), take us up."

AND NOW WE BEGIN THE ADVENTURES OF HELICOPTER JIM!

And so (HELICOPTER NAME) takes them all up... close to where the battle is happening.

HJ: "Princess Eva, use your chain, to at least slow down Fury as well as to see what the chain can do."

MIKHAIL: "I'll be safe. I have liquid metal as my armor, so I...I'll be fine."

SCOTT: "I'll keep using my InvisiBow, but I'm not sure what kind of damage this will do."

And Blue sends off another ball of ice and a huge one too. At the same time, Blue flaps its wings towards Fury.

And as the ball of ice is flying towards Fury, as Helicopter Jim and the rest of the team get closer to Fury, Blue flaps his wing and sends off enough power to break apart the ice, the ball of ice and all of the tiny particles hit Fury. And once again, does a lot of damage. While Fury is trying to regain control of flying in the air, Princess Eva throws the chain towards Fury.

And as she does so, Mr. Cape shoots a couple arrows at the chain to give it more speed so that it can go towards Fury. And as the chain is heading towards Fury, the chain never ends. Princess Eva is looking at the chain in her hand while the chain is going out. And she's looking at Scott and Scott is looking at her.

SCOTT: "I guess we know now what the chain is able to do. That's like a never ending chain."

And so the chain goes towards Fury and is able to wrap around the neck area part of Fury. Princess Eva latches the chain to (HELICOPTER NAME). And now they're able to hold Fury. Blue is striking Fury, ice ball after ice ball, and Fury shoots a fireball. It's heading straight towards (HELICOPTER NAME).

HELICOPTER: "Hang on everyone. This is going to be a major hit."

And (HELICOPTER NAME) just holds its ground and takes the hit...(EXPLOSION SOUND F/X)

And Helicopter Jim transforms (HELICOPTER NAME) into a different form, which is able to be quicker for this battle. And (HELICOPTER NAME) is able to move quicker because Jim transformed (HELICOPTER NAME) into a different shape. And now they look more like a jet.

HJ: "Let's fly around to the other side and let's tie-up Fury with the chain."

And so they go around and around Fury.

And as they're doing so, Mikhail jumps out of (HELICOPTER NAME) with the power staff, clothed with liquid metal as his armor and is heading straight toward Fury.

HJ: "Mikhail! What are you doing?"

And Mikhail is heading straight towards Fury. And as he gets closer to Fury, he takes his power staff and strikes Fury right on the neck. Fury lets off a big screech (EAGLE SCREECH). Mikhail quickly grabs a hold of the chain that is around Fury and is holding on.

MIKHAIL: "Mr. Cape, shoot an arrow. I'll catch it...and when I do, direct the arrow to come back to (HELICOPTER NAME)."

So Mr. Cape does what Mikhail tells him to do. He shoots a

smart arrow, directs it to go towards Mikhail and it does. Mikhail catches the arrow and hangs on for dear life. And Mr. Cape brings the arrow back to the helicopter and (HELICOPTER NAME) opens its side panel and Mikhail is able to return back. And Fury is now weakened.

HJ: "Okay, guys, now that we have Fury wrapped in this chain, we're gonna have to be quick about this. And if we can do it like how Mikhail just did it, we can all go one by one. And we're gonna have to do our very best to take out Fury. I'm gonna go now, I'm gonna… my turn…it's my turn."

So Helicopter Jim jumps out of (HELICOPTER NAME).

And because they're above Fury, as Blue continues with ice ball after ice ball, Fury is becoming weaker by each shot Blue takes. And as Helicopter Jim is heading toward Fury, he takes out his sword and as he gets closer, he strikes Fury on his wing (EXPLOSION), one of Fury's wings is now damaged. And as Jim is falling, Mr. Cape shoots an infinite arrow, a smart arrow toward Jim…and Jim catches the arrow.

Mr. Cape is able to bring Jim back to the helicopter. Zaiah jumps out, strikes Fury in the other wing… on his other wing with his Power Sword. His other wing is now damaged. Fury cannot fly as well as he did before. Blue continues to bring major damage to Fury, ice ball after ice ball.

SCOTT: "Finally, it's my turn."

Scott takes out his InvisiBow and strikes Fury with so many arrows that Fury lets off a loud shriek (SHRIEK IN PAIN).

HJ: "Guys, we gotta end this. Blue, it's your turn Blue! Do

what you gotta do."

Just then, Blue looks at Mikhail, and Mikhail says to Princess Eva...

MIKHAIL: "Princess Eva, Blue needs you to let go of Fury. He needs you to release him from the chain."

PRINCESS EVA: "What!? What's gonna happen though? If I release him from the chain...what if he gets... what if he becomes free?"

MIKHAIL: "You have to trust me, trust that Blue needs you to do that."

And so Princess Eva, with one whip of the chain is able to let Fury free from the grasp of the chain. Just then...

AND THAT WILL BE THE NEXT ADVENTURE OF HELICOPTER JIM.

Adventure 140

On the last adventure of Helicopter Jim, Mikhail, Jim, Zaiah, Scott, and Mr. Cape is helping Blue as he battles Fury. Princess Eva has Fury wrapped up in the chain and she's hanging on tightly to it...

MIKHAIL: "Princess Eva, Blue needs you to let go of Fury. He needs you to release him from the chain."

PRINCESS EVA: "What!? What's gonna happen though? If I release him from the chain...what if he gets... what if he becomes free?"

MIKHAIL: "You have to trust me, trust that Blue needs you to do that."

And so Princess Eva, with one whip of the chain is able to let Fury free from the grasp of the chain. Just then...

AND NOW WE BEGIN THE ADVENTURES OF HELICOPTER JIM!

Just then, Blue speeds up and flies towards Fury... as fast as he can towards Fury.

Fury regains some strength and Fury is having a hard time flying because of his damaged wings and Fury lets off a loud shriek (SHRIEK), and sends off another fireball. But Blue is flying so fast that he goes right through the fireball and heads straight towards Fury. Fury lets off another shriek (SHRIEK) and so does Blue (SHRIEK). And Blue crashes right into Fury. And as he does so, a huge explosion takes place. (EXPLOSION). And it's so bright that they can't see what happened.

Helicopter Jim and the rest of the team, while protected in (HELICOPTER NAME), can't see because it's so bright. (HELICOPTER NAME) gets hit also from the shockwave from the explosion and tumbles in the air, but Jim is able to regain control.

HJ: "Okay, whoa that was close... is everybody okay?"

ZAIAH: "Yes, we're fine."

Helicopter Jim is looking for Blue and he can't find Blue. And he's wondering if Blue is okay.

HJ: "Does anybody see Blue? (HELICOPTER NAME), can you... can you scan for Blue?"

HELICOPTER: "I already tried... I can't find Blue anywhere.'"

Just then Helicopter Jim sees a bright blue glow falling in the sky. It is June...

HJ: "(HELICOPTER NAME), we need to... we need to catch that. That's June falling, go get it (HELICOPTER NAME)."

And so (HELICOPTER NAME) sweeps under the Stone and Jim is able to catch the Stone of June.

Helicopter Jim lands (HELICOPTER NAME), and it's raining. There's still some thunder. lightning and rain. Helicopter Jim is wondering what just happened. Is that it? And as it continues to rain, Helicopter Jim notices that the rain is not just any rain. There's...there's normal rain, but then he sees blue raindrops and he's wondering what just happened.

Helicopter Jim notices that as it's raining, in the rain, he sees a formation with all the blue rain coming together and it reshapes into Blue. And as it reshapes into Blue, Blue is falling from the sky and lands on the ground with a loud slam, (SLAMMING THE GROUND SOUND), and Helicopter Jim runs over to Blue and puts his hands on Blue's chest...

HJ: (SAD AND CONCERNED) "Blue...Blue...c'mon Blue..."

PRINCESS EVA: "I'm so sorry Jim."

SCOTT: "Awe man... Jim...I'm so sorry."

Everyone is saddened...

As they're walking back to (HELICOPTER NAME), Jim remembers something...

HJ: (MUMBLING UNDER HIS BREATH) "Wait a minute...June is able to bring Blue to life..."

And Helicopter Jim is wondering if he's still able to do that.

He runs toward Blue's head and sees the area where the eye is, where his eye is. Jim takes the Stone of June and places it in the eye of Blue. And, all of a sudden, Jim sees Blue's wing move a little...then his foot... then Blue's eyes begin to glow...life is restored back to Blue. Blue gets up, flaps his wings a little, shakes off some of the water and some of the debris that's on him, and lets off a loud screech (EAGLE SCREECH).

HJ: "You're alive!!"

MIKHAIL: "Hey, Jim, that's Blue saying thank you. And to all of us, Blue said, 'Well done!'"

HJ: "You too Blue, well done! That… was incredible!"

AND THAT WILL BE THE NEXT ADVENTURE OF HELICOPTER JIM.

Adventure 141

On the last adventure of Helicopter Jim, Blue gave Fury the final blow, which ended the battle with a huge explosion. June is falling in the sky and Helicopter Jim is able to capture it. Blue is reformed from all of the blue rain that's falling.

Blue lands on the ground and has no life left in him...Blue is dead.

Everyone is saddened...

As they're walking back to (HELICOPTER NAME), Jim remembers something...

HJ: (MUMBLING UNDER HIS BREATH) "Wait a minute...June is able to bring Blue to life..."

And Helicopter Jim is wondering if he's still able to do that.

He runs toward Blue's head and sees the area where the eye is, where his eye is. Jim takes the Stone of June and places it in the eye of Blue. And, all of a sudden, Jim sees Blue's wing move a little...then his foot... then Blue's eyes begin to glow...life is restored back to Blue. Blue gets up, flaps his wings a little, shakes off some of the water and some of the debris that's on him, and lets off a loud screech (EAGLE SCREECH).

HJ: "You're alive!!"

MIKHAIL: "Hey, Jim, that's Blue saying thank you. And to all of us, Blue said, 'Well done!'"

HJ: "You too Blue, well done! That... was incredible!"

AND NOW WE BEGIN THE ADVENTURES OF

HELICOPTER JIM!

HJ: "Hey guys, we need to get back to the barrier as quickly as possible. We don't know what happened to Fury, if he's destroyed, if he's still alive, we don't... we don't know what's happening, so we need to get out of here quickly."

Mr. Cape and Mikhail agreed, they knew about Fury better than any of the others on the team. So, Helicopter Jim jumped into (HELICOPTER NAME), and got everybody else to jump in too.

HJ: "Blue, we're gonna go to the barrier where my father is. I'm not sure if Fury is still around, and if he does show up, you know what to do."

And Blue flapped his wings, nodded his head and scratched the ground with his claws...

MIKHAIL: "That means he's ready."

And so they all jumped into (HELICOPTER NAME) and they headed back to the barrier.

SCOTT: (WITH WIDE EYES) "That was... incredibly scary, but at the same time... victorious! I mean, that was... that was so cool, Princess, how you used the chain. And it's... it's amazing how the chain works. I mean, look at it, it's... it's just, uh, it just looks like a... like a...a rope. It doesn't even look that strong, that's so amazing. I guess the Mighty 3 were correct. These... the gear that they gave to us is amazing."

PRINCESS EVA: "Yeah, I was amazed at what it was able to do, but the smart arrow, that was pretty interesting."

HJ: "Yeah, that...that was, I mean, that was genius Mikhail

for you to think about that. But I think if we all work together, we can accomplish much. So as we head to the barrier, we have to think through what we need to do because if Fury does show up, we have to be ready for him."

And so, as they're heading back to the barrier, as they're getting closer and closer Jim is wondering...

HJ: "Hey, Mikhail, I have a question. Why is it when... remember at Lava City when I was in the process of retrieving March, that when I fell off of the butterfly, you came under me as a stream of water and I was able to stand on you because I had the Stone of February?"

MIKHAIL: "Yes."

HJ: "But I wasn't holding February... I thought I needed to hold the Stone in order to use it. February was in my pouch and yet I was able to be on the water. I don't... I don't get it."

MIKHAIL: "Here's what you need to know... the Stones that are used to make decisions, like January, need to be held, because you're making a decision. And because you have to make a decision, you have to intentionally hold the Stone. For Stones like February, which is to walk on water, that can happen whether or not you make a decision to do so. Yet, if you want to go under water, February will recognize it and you'll be able to go under. The Stone of May is another Stone where you need to make a decision... like bringing healing. When you use the Stone of May, you're gonna bring healing to someone... You're making a decision, so you need to be holding that Stone."

SCOTT: "Well, that's a detail we should have said earlier. That...that...that's not just some *minor* thing you leave out of the instructions."

MIKHAIL: "Yes... true Scott, I apologize for that. There are many details that come with being responsible for these Stones, as well as a lot that we're gonna learn together along this journey because there are so many complex situations that we don't know of that we will probably learn along the way. I mean, just think of the Book of Life. Look at how... look at how thick it is! There...there are so many things in there that I'm sure we can learn from."

PRINCESS EVA: "Yeah, Scott, while we're heading to the barrier, why don't you go ahead and open it up and start reading some of it, you might learn a thing or two."

SCOTT: "Yeah, I...I'll get to it, that's a lot of reading. Maybe I'll... maybe I'll read a couple of pages."

AND THAT WILL BE THE NEXT ADVENTURE OF HELICOPTER JIM.

Adventure 142

On the last adventure of Helicopter Jim, (HELICOPTER NAME), Jim, Mr. Cape, Mikhail, Princess Eva, Scott, and Blue the Giant Eagle, were getting ready to go to the barrier. They just finished the battle with Fury and were celebrating the victory.

Jim asked some questions regarding the Stones...and so Mikhail did his best to explain to Jim about the Stones...

MIKHAIL: "Here's what you need to know... the Stones that are used to make decisions, like January, need to be held, because you're making a decision. And because you have to make a decision, you have to intentionally hold the Stone. For Stones like February, which is to walk on water, that can happen whether or not you make a decision to do so. Yet, if you want to go under water, February will recognize it and you'll be able to go under. The Stone of May is another Stone where you need to make a decision... like bringing healing. When you use the Stone of May, you're gonna bring healing to someone... You're making a decision, so you need to be holding that Stone."

SCOTT: "Well, that's a detail we should have said earlier. That...that...that's not just some *minor* thing you leave out of the instructions."

MIKHAIL: "Yes... true Scott, I apologize for that. There are many details that come with being responsible for these Stones, as well as a lot that we're gonna learn together along this journey because there are so many complex situations that we don't know of that we will probably learn along the way. I mean, just think of the Book of Life. Look at how... look at how thick it is!

There...there are so many things in there that I'm sure we can learn from."

PRINCESS EVA: "Yeah, Scott, while we're heading to the barrier, why don't you go ahead and open it up and start reading some of it, you might learn a thing or two."

SCOTT: "Yeah, I...I'll get to it, that's a lot of reading. Maybe I'll... maybe I'll read a couple of pages."

AND NOW WE BEGIN THE ADVENTURES OF HELICOPTER JIM!

MR. CAPE: "You know, one thing is for sure Jim, is that as much as we do know, there are probably more things we do not know, and this is where you need to trust in being the Chosen One. That even though we don't have all the information or the exact type of information that you would really want or that you would learn about after something happens, you're just gonna have to be okay with it because it comes with being the Chosen One."

ZAIAH: "You know something, the emperor always told me that just because you have this responsibility doesn't mean you know everything that comes with the responsibility. Majority of what you're going to learn with who you are is while you're on the journey of becoming who you're supposed to be."

HELICOPTER: "As much as I know, there is still much for me to learn even though all that you're going through is tough for you."

Just then they were approaching the barrier and (HELICOPTER NAME) did a quick scan and Fury was nowhere to be found.

HJ: "I'm gonna go in and when I do, I don't know what my dad is gonna talk to me about. But I think you guys will be okay, you have Blue, we have each other, we have all the gear and equipment from the Mighty 3... so let's stand guard and let's see where we go from here."

And so (HELICOPTER NAME) approached the barrier... Helicopter Jim exited the helicopter and approached the barrier.

All of a sudden, right in front of him appears... the Dark Hood leader. Helicopter Jim was startled, and didn't know that the Dark Hood leader would appear that quickly.

HJ: "Whoa, where'd you come from? What... h...how'd you even get here that fast? Where were you? I didn't even see you."

DH LEADER: "I am the gatekeeper to the barrier. So, when anyone approaches, I can instantly get here."

HJ: "Whoa, that's so cool."

DH LEADER: "Are you ready, Jim?"

HJ: "Yes, I am."

DH LEADER: "Once you go through, take your time. But when I am ready to open the gate, I will light up the barrier. And at that point, you can come through the gate."

So, Helicopter Jim was ready to go in. The Dark Hood leader opened the gate, and Helicopter Jim went right through it. And he was on the other side of the barrier. The Dark Hood leader closed the gate behind Helicopter Jim, and Jim found himself in a place that he has never felt before. It was empty and void.

There were no walls, no floor, no ceiling, nothing in there. He was in open space. And as he's looking around, he doesn't see anything or anyone. He doesn't even see his father.

Helicopter Jim begins to believe that maybe this was a trap, and he doesn't know what to do.

HJ: "Dad? Hey, Dad. Are you around here? Are you in here? Dad?"

And nothing. Helicopter Jim felt alone once again.

Just then, far off, distant from where he is, Jim sees a tiny white glow. And he's wondering what that is. The glow comes closer to him and closer and closer. And now it's so bright, he can't even look at it. And the glow comes right before him, and it is so bright that Helicopter Jim cannot even see, and all he hears is a voice.

JS: "My son."

HJ: "Is that… is that you, Dad?"

JS: "Jim, I've waited for so long to see you. I'm sorry things are turning out this way."

HJ: "Dad… is that you?"

JS: "Yes, son. It's me… but you cannot see me right now."

HJ: "Why...why… what is… why are you so bright?"

JS: "Well, there's...there's something that you need to know. And I'm sure you've been learning along the way about being the Chosen One."

HJ: (EMOTIONALLY DOWN) "Well, there is a lot that I'm learning. You know, the people that I'm with...and, of course,

Scott being here...uh, things are... things are difficult at times, but I...I...I do wanna see you, Dad. I...I...I wanna hug you, I wanna... I miss you. I thought something happened to you, so I didn't know... I didn't even know what to think when I got in here. And now, I can't... I can't even see you or...or...or...or feel you or...or touch you. It's just... it's...it's... I didn't think it was going to be like this."

JS: "I know Jim. I know. But in due time, in time, we'll be able to be together again, the way we were."

HJ: "Uh, so, what is this place? Why...why are you even in here?"

AND THAT WILL BE THE NEXT ADVENTURE OF HELICOPTER JIM.

Adventure 143

On the last adventure of Helicopter Jim, Jim, Scott, Princess Eva, Mikhail, Mr. Cape, (HELICOPTER NAME) and Blue were at the barrier. The Dark Hood Leader, who was the gatekeeper of the barrier, opened the gate for Jim. Everyone was waiting for Jim outside of the barrier as Jim entered the barrier to see his father.

HJ: "Dad… is that you?"

JS: "Yes, son. It's me… but you cannot see me right now."

HJ: "Why...why… what is… why are you so bright?"

JS: "Well, there's...there's something that you need to know. And I'm sure you've been learning along the way about being the Chosen One."

HJ: (EMOTIONALLY DOWN) "Well, there is a lot that I'm learning. You know, the people that I'm with...and, of course, Scott being here...uh, things are… things are difficult at times, but I...I...I do wanna see you, Dad. I...I...I wanna hug you, I wanna… I miss you. I thought something happened to you, so I didn't know… I didn't even know what to think when I got in here. And now, I can't… I can't even see you or...or...or...or feel you or...or touch you. It's just… it's...it's… I didn't think it was going to be like this."

JS: "I know Jim. I know. But in due time, in time, we'll be able to be together again, the way we were."

HJ: "Uh, so, what is this place? Why...why are you even in here?"

AND NOW WE BEGIN THE ADVENTURES OF HELICOPTER JIM!

JS: "Dayor wants nothing more than for you to be destroyed. And he'll stop at nothing, including trying to get to me to get to you. So, when I received that phone call, before all of this began, I was given notice that you were the Chosen One. All throughout history, we always knew that the Chosen One would be the One to bring peace to the entire universe. We just didn't know who exactly the Chosen One would be. But we did have an idea that the Chosen One would come from the family of one of the Kings...we also knew what was to be required of the Chosen One. So, when I found out that you were the Chosen One, I got alarmed a little, because I know what you need to go through in order to bring peace to the entire universe, and it hurts my heart."

HJ: "I know Dad. There's...there's... I mean, there's so many things that...that I'm learning, and...and risks that are being taken... but if I am the Chosen One, which I know I am by now, I mean, there are things that I didn't think I were... that I was capable of... of accomplishing. I mean, we're... we're... we're... we're doing great, Dad. I have such a great team around me. And then, of course, the helicopter, I mean, what a gift. You know, we named it, too."

JS: "Really? What did you name it?"

HJ: "Well, we named it (HELICOPTER NAME)."

JS: "That is the perfect name! But know this Jim, that even though you may have gone through many difficulties, I am always there with you. I will always be there with you. Right now though, you need to do this without me. And there is a reason for it that I cannot explain to you right now. But you need to trust me. That for this next part of your journey, which will be the most difficult part, you're going to have to persevere through it. As difficult as it will be, in the end, it will all work out together for good. You just need to believe that."

HJ: "I do believe that Dad. I really do. I just wish you could… you could be with us and...and come with us. But I do trust that...that you need to do what you need to do. And I'll be okay, Dad. I'll be okay."

JS: "That's my boy. I knew you would. I knew that you would find good people to surround yourself with. And I know, at an early age, you're doing things that you never thought you would be doing, but I believe in you. I know that as the Chosen One, you will be able to accomplish great things, even more than any ordinary person. You are someone who is extraordinary."

Just then, the Dark Hood leader lit up the place signifying that it was time for Jim to exit the barrier.

JS: "Well, there… that's your... that's your sign. That's your exit."

HJ: "Dad, I...I...I really wish you could come with us."

JS: "I know Jim. I know. I can't go with you physically, but take this with you."

HJ: "Take what?"

JS: "Well… just open your hand."

Helicopter Jim opened his hand, and there was a small tiny little jewel, a clear jewel. It looked like a diamond.

HJ: "Wh...what do I do with this?"

JS: "Give it to (HELICOPTER NAME)."

HJ: "Okay. I'll...I'll do that. I'm sure (HELICOPTER NAME) would know what to do with it, right?"

JS: "Absolutely."

HJ: "Okay."

JS: "Don't worry. You'll be okay, Jim."

HJ: "I know, Dad."

JS: "You better go now. There's a lot for you to accomplish. Go get them Stones. I believe in you, son. Go get 'em!"

Helicopter Jim exited the barrier and the Dark Hood leader closed the gate.

HJ: "Thank you. I appreciate it. Until we see each other again."

Helicopter Jim went back into (HELICOPTER NAME), and Helicopter Jim looked at everyone, and they're all wondering what happened.

SCOTT: "Hey... Jim, are you okay?"

HJ: "Yeah. Yeah, I'm good."

PRINCESS EVA: "Were you able to see your father?"

HJ: (A LITTLE SAD) "No, not...not really. Um, not...no. Not him, but I was able to speak with him. It was just...just a bright light that came toward me, um, but no, I-I-I wasn't able to see him."

MR. CAPE: "Jim, it's okay. There's a reason, and in the end, you'll understand why, but for now, just trust."

HJ: "No, I...I do, I do. Mr. Cape, I trust my dad. In fact, he gave me this...this jewel, uh, to give to (HELICOPTER NAME)."

MIKHAIL: "That...that is the... that is the (SNAPPING FINGERS THINKING) Crystal, uh, that is the... Crystal of Life. That is... that's a good thing! Yeah. I'm glad that... I'm glad that your father gave you that."

ZAIAH: "What is the Crystal of Life?"

MIKHAIL: "Give it to (HELICOPTER NAME). Put it... You see that-that compartment right there. Put it right there."

HELICOPTER: "Jim, I know what to do with that. I know what that is. And yes, do exactly what Mikhail said. Put it right there."

And so Helicopter Jim put the Crystal of Life in this tiny little compartment, and (HELICOPTER NAME) took it, and then all of a sudden…

AND THAT WILL BE THE NEXT ADVENTURE OF HELICOPTER JIM.

Adventure 144

On the last adventure of Helicopter Jim, Jim's father gave him a small tiny little clear jewel that looked like a diamond to give to (HELICOPTER NAME).

MIKHAIL: "That...that is the... that is the (SNAPPING FINGERS THINKING) Crystal, uh, that is the... Crystal of Life. That is... that's a good thing! Yeah. I'm glad that... I'm glad that your father gave you that."

ZAIAH: "What is the Crystal of Life?"

MIKHAIL: "Give it to (HELICOPTER NAME). Put it... You see that-that compartment right there. Put it right there."

HELICOPTER: "Jim, I know what to do with that. I know what that is. And yes, do exactly what Mikhail said. Put it right there."

And so Helicopter Jim put the Crystal of Life in this tiny little compartment, and (HELICOPTER NAME) took it, and then all of a sudden...

AND NOW WE BEGIN THE ADVENTURES OF HELICOPTER JIM!

And all of a sudden...Jim's dad spoke...

JS: "Hey, Jimmy!"

HJ: "Dad, dad, is that you?"

JS: "Yeah, it's me."

HJ: "What...what are you... What is this?"

JS: "That's the Crystal of Life. You're now connected to me.

You'll be able to communicate with me as if I was there with you, but only through (HELICOPTER NAME). That's what the Crystal of Life does. It gives you access to me, and it gives me access to you."

HJ: "That's the coolest thing Dad! That-that is unbelievable! I'm so thankful. I'm so glad. I'm so happy! You can be with us! You can be with me!"

JS: "Yep. I told you Jimmy, It'll all work out together for good."

HJ: "Okay, Dad. Well, right now, we have to search for... we have to search for the Stone of September."

JS: "Oh, you're... September. Okay. Well, apparently, it seems you have a couple of other "gems" with you...and so, who's with you?"

MR. CAPE: "It's me, Mr. Cape."

JS: "Aaaah…. I'm so glad that you guys are together. Who else is with you, Jim?"

MIKHAIL: "It's me, Mikhail."

JS: "Thank you. Thank you so much for taking good care of Jim."

MIKHAIL: "You're welcome. You're welcome."

HJ: "We also have...we also have, uh, Zaiah."

JS: "Zaiah? Is he with the emperor?"

HJ: "Yeah. Yes, he is. How do you know that?"

JS: "Well, there's only one Zaiah that the emperor talks

195

about. And I'm sure that he's the one. By the way, did you get to meet the emperor's daughter? She's about your age."

PRINCESS EVA: "Yes, he did...I'm here."

JS: "Ooooh, Princess, you were able to come along the journey?"

PRINCESS EVA: "Yes, I...I am. I am able. I...I wish I could meet you, but I guess it's nice to meet you even in this way."

JS: "It's...it's nice to hear, you. It's nice to hear you. Um, you must be grown up by now. You know, the last time I saw you, you were just a baby."

PRINCESS: "Really? Oh, that's...I didn't...I didn't know that you saw me."

JS: "Yep. I was there when you were just a little baby."

SCOTT: "That is so cool. So, a lot of people know you. How...how is this possible? Is there something that I'm missing?"

JS: "Scott, there is a lot that we all are learning. But we'll be able to catch up later with all the details. For now, there's a lot of work to do. And I'm thankful to you too Scott. Thank you for your bravery and...and making sure that Jim is okay. I knew you guys would do well together."

HJ: "Okay. Well, let's look for September. We know it's here, on Diamond Crust."

So, Helicopter Jim and the rest of the team headed out in search of the Stone of September. Helicopter Jim was wondering what direction they should go, because there are so many options, so many different areas they could go. And Helicopter

Jim took out January just for Wisdom. And Wisdom said they needed to see the Seer. And the only way they could see the Seer was to go to the Cave of Faith.

HJ: "Hey, Zaiah...do you know where the Cave of Faith is around here?"

ZAIAH: "The Cave of Faith? I've never heard of the Cave of Faith."

PRINCESS: "I...I have."

ZAIAH: "You have?"

PRINCESS EVA: "Yes. From a very young age, my...my father always told me that there is a Cave of Faith...and there may come a day where I will need to know where this certain cave is. And he told me, it was the Cave of Faith. I didn't know what he meant. He just said I will need to know where it is. So, he showed me the area where the cave is located...but couldn't show me the cave because no one can see it."

ZAIAH: "That's okay. So, where do we go?"

PRINCESS EVA: "Well, he showed me the area. I don't know how he got there. I was so small."

ZAIAH: "Well, explain what the surroundings were like."

PRINCESS EVA: "Well, I do remember... I do remember there were, of course, high cliffs."

ZAIAH: "Was it... was it rock cliffs? Was it... wa...was there trees? Were there... Wha...wha...wha...what was your surrounding like? Was it cold? Was it hot?"

PRINCESS EVA: "I know it wasn't cold, but it wasn't really

hot. I mean, it wasn't... it wasn't warm either. It was more on the hotter side, but it wasn't too hot."

ZAIAH: "And not too many trees?"

PRINCESS EVA: "No, not too many trees, but toward the evening, it did get cloudy. I noticed that, and I just remembered that night, it...it got cold."

ZAIAH: "Okay. Well, it...it seems like you're describing The Outlands, and that may be the place."

HELICOPTER: "I'm already on it Zaiah..."

ZAIAH: "The Outlands. Let me see the map (HELICOPTER NAME). Let me see the map."

And so, (HELICOPTER NAME) put the map on the screen.

ZAIAH: "Okay. So, here...here's where we are. That is... that's us right there?"

HELICOPTER: "Yes. That dot right there blinking, that is us."

ZAIAH: "Okay, there's Diamond Falls. This is where we just came from. Okay, that... and that's the Swamplands. Okay, The Outlands are over here in this direction right there. That's...that's The Outlands."

HJ: "Well, according to this map, that...that river right there, it goes all the way to Diamond Falls.

ZAIAH: "Yeah, that's the... that's the Diamond River. The Diamond River feeds all of the land. That is the main water source for everything. But that's where we need to go. It's...it's... and in that area, there are a lot of waterfalls. So...but that's the area we need to go to."

HJ: "Well, that's where we're gonna go. So, let's go (HELICOPTER NAME)."

AND THAT WILL BE THE NEXT ADVENTURE OF HELICOPTER JIM.

Adventure 145

On the last adventure of Helicopter Jim, Jim told his dad who he was with and his father knew who they were. Jim wanted to search for September next, so he used January for wisdom to see if he could locate September, and wisdom said he needed to see the Seer. So Jim asked Zaiah if he knew where the Cave of Faith was...but he didn't...but Princess Eva did. She explained to Zaiah what she remembered about the area and Zaiah was able to get an idea of where the Cave of Faith might be. (HELICOPTER NAME) pulled up the map of the area for all of them to see...

ZAIAH: "Okay, there's Diamond Falls. This is where we just came from. Okay, that... and that's the Swamplands. Okay, The Outlands are over here in this direction right there. That's...that's The Outlands."

HJ: "Well, according to this map, that...that river right there, it goes all the way to Diamond Falls.

ZAIAH: "Yeah, that's the... that's the Diamond River. The Diamond River feeds all of the land. That is the main water source for everything. But that's where we need to go. It's...it's... and in that area, there are a lot of waterfalls. So...but that's the area we need to go to."

HJ: "Well, that's where we're gonna go. So, let's go (HELICOPTER NAME)."

AND NOW WE BEGIN THE ADVENTURES OF HELICOPTER JIM!

So they headed into the direction of The Outlands. As they got closer to The Outlands Helicopter Jim noticed that everyone was a little nervous about September and all that they've been through.

JS: "Hey, Jim, you know, September...although September has its fair share of power, September is a very unique stone because it empowers. It's able to restore power to any Stone. Because of that uniqueness, September is probably one of the hardest Stones to take possession of, but I know you'll be able to do it."

SCOTT: "Yeah, I...I...I believe you can too. I've seen you do amazing things Jim. So, we got this."

HELICOPTER: "We're approaching the area. And as much as I can tell, there are a lot of waterfalls Jim. So, we're going to have to be careful about this. There are a lot of areas where there are rapid rivers. So, just be careful. And the temperature of the waters are very cold. So, you don't want to fall in lest you freeze or get hypothermia."

HJ: "Well, then I'm just going to... gonna have to rely on all of you, like I've been doing, but we can do this."

So, Helicopter Jim and the rest of the team got closer to The Outlands and the falls and Diamond River.

HELICOPTER: "I'm going to land in that area right there."

And so, (HELICOPTER NAME) brings them into an area where it is filled and surrounded with waterfalls...very tall waterfalls.

Helicopter Jim steps out of (HELICOPTER NAME). And everyone else steps out.

HJ: "Hey, Dad, you know, I...I know you're not able to come

with me, but we're gonna head out and...and...and search for the Cave of Faith, but I'll be back. And...and, um, so, know that we'll be okay."

JS: "I know Jim, I know you'll be okay."

So, Helicopter Jim and the rest of the team headed out to look for the Cave of Faith.

SCOTT: "Okay, so how are we gonna do this? We're gonna split up? What are we... what are we gonna do? Uh, because we know that it's a... it's a cave, so it has to be somewhere along the mountain sides."

HJ: "Well, we're assuming that. I mean, the Cave of Faith could be anywhere. Princess Eva, do you... do you remember anything in this area?

PRINCESS EVA: (FOCUSED THINKING) "No, we're in the right area. I remember these waterfalls. I remember all of it. I...I do remember... I do remember my dad picking me up and put... he put me on his... on his shoulders. I think he did that because he crossed... he crossed the water. I think he went across the river. I think we have to cross somewhere around there. If you go in that area...do you see right next to tha...that waterfall? I mean, that's the... that area looks very familiar. It's a flat... a flat area, but I think there are caves in that area. So I... I'd say let's go in that... in that area. It...it looks fine to me. We're just gonna have to cross over, uh, through the water."

SCOTT: "Well, all I know, from what (HELICOPTER NAME) has said, is that the water is freezing. So, we're gonna have to cross over quickly, maybe make a fire and then warm ourselves up. So, if...if we're gonna do that, I'm good with that, but I ain't staying in no wet clothes so that I freeze. So long as we make a fire."

MR. CAPE: "You'll be fine, Scott. We'll...we'll do this together."

MIKHAIL: "You know, this place is very calm. But don't...don't let the calmness fool you. It...it sounds relaxing with the waterfalls, the river, the water. But there's just something about this place that...that doesn't seem calm."

SCOTT: (CONCERNED) "Wait a minute, what...what are you doing? Why are you saying that? Now you're scaring me. What are you... what are you trying to say?"

MIKHAIL: "No, it's... Just be careful, just be cautious. Like Jim's dad was saying, "September is gonna be a difficult Stone to get. So, it's...all that we're gonna be doing, even though it seems easy, can become difficult."

SCOTT: "Okay, I...I get that. We'll just keep our eyes open."

HJ: "Yeah, let's just be cautious, guys. So, let's... let's cross... let's cross the river."

So, they all walked towards the river, to an area where they could cross over.

As soon as they got to water, something changed, and they all noticed it. It's like the temperature dropped, and the atmosphere around them became a little darker.

SCOTT: "Whoa, okay. I'm sure you all sense that and see that, something changed."

MIKHAIL: "Yeah, I...I feel it. There's something...

something's happening right now. And I don't know what it is."

MR. CAPE: "Mikhail, I think it has something to do with just this area specifically. I think... I think it's because the Cave of Faith might be around here. It's also a place where Dayor might have set things up."

HJ: "Wait... What a min... wait a minute. What do you mean, set things up?"

AND THAT WILL BE THE NEXT ADVENTURE OF HELICOPTER JIM.

Adventure 146

On the last adventure of Helicopter Jim, Jim, Scott, Princess Eva, Mr. Cape, Mikhail, and Zaiah, along with Blue, were in search of the Cave of Faith to see the Seer, hoping the Seer would help them locate the Stone of September.

Princess Eva vaguely remembers the area where the Cave of Faith might be located, but she remembered just enough to get them close by. They travel to Diamond River, which is the main water source for the entire land. As they exit (HELICOPTER NAME), they need to cross the river to get to where she felt the cave might be.

So they all walked towards the river, to an area where they could cross over.

As soon as they got to water, something changed, and they all noticed it. It's like the temperature dropped, and the atmosphere around them became a little darker.

SCOTT: "Whoa, okay. I'm sure you all sense that and see that, something changed."

MIKHAIL: "Yeah, I...I feel it. There's something... something's happening right now. And I don't know what it is."

MR. CAPE: "Mikhail, I think it has something to do with just this area specifically. I think... I think it's because the Cave of Faith might be around here. It's also a place where Dayor might have set things up."

HJ: "Wait... What a min... wait a minute. What do you mean, set things up?"

AND NOW WE BEGIN THE ADVENTURES OF HELICOPTER JIM!

MIKHAIL: "I sense something. There's definitely something around here, and I cannot figure out what it is."

HJ: "Well, the-the best we can do is start crossing the river."

And so, one by one, they all stepped into water, starting with Mr. Cape.

SCOTT: "Wait a minute, why are... why are we walking *through* the...the...the water? Jim, you have the Stone of February. Let's use February."

HJ: "That's right. I didn't even think about that."

SCOTT: "How could you not think about that?"

HJ: "Well, I'm...I'm getting used to using the different Stones okay? So, I...I... Give me a break...okay? It's not like I-I always have them on my mind. I have to think about these things. Okay? But now we know so... and...and we can... we can do this."

SCOTT: "Of course we can...just calm down a bit buddy!"

HJ: "Okay, guys, just stay near me, that's all you have to do and you'll be fine."

So, Helicopter Jim started to walk on the water.

Princess Eva followed after him.

PRINCESS EVA: "This is so cool. This is unbelievable. This is... this is the coolest thing."

SCOTT: "Yep, this... this is... I love it. This is so good!"

And as he's walking on the water, Scott notices something

unique about the water...

SCOTT: "Look at how clear the water is. I can see the bottom. And, in fact, the bottom looks kind of weird, like there's a mirror. It looks like silver. That's interesting."

MR. CAPE: "Yes, this is... this is incredible, much better than falling in and... and getting hypothermia."

ZAIAH: "You know, I...I do this a lot. So, I... You know, it's...it's normal for me to be walking like this."

SCOTT: (WITH A JOKING ATTITUDE) "Yeah, good for you, Zaiah. We're not *all* like you. So, can you just, you know, let us *enjoy* this moment Mr. (IMITATES ZAIAH) 'You know I do this a lot...it's normal for me.' I'm glad *you* can walk on water. Unlike us, we need Jim and the Stone of February."

As they're walking, Mikhail stops...

SCOTT: "What... why are you stopping? Keep walking... What are you doing?"

Mikhail closes his eyes and stands still in the middle of the river.

SCOTT: "Hey, guys-guys stop. Wait a... Hang on. What is Mikhail doing?"

Jim turned around...

HJ: "Mikhail, are you okay? Mikhail...Mikhail...hey."

Mikhail didn't move. He didn't say anything. He just stood there with his eyes closed.

MR. CAPE: "Hey, Jim, I think Mikhail senses something. So, I think he's just getting a reading of the land and what's taking place. So, let him be, he'll be okay. I'm sure he's gonna give us an assessment of the land as soon as he's able to."

Just then the waters began to bubble up and begin to look like it was boiling, but it wasn't hot. Something was stirring within all of the waters around them. The waterfalls became more rapid.

Helicopter Jim didn't know what was going on. The water that they were standing on began to bubble also. And Helicopter Jim doesn't know what's happening.

MR. CAPE: "Jim, something is definitely wrong. We need to get to the cave quickly."

HJ: "But what do we do with Mikhail? He's just standing there."

MR. CAPE: "He'll be fine."

ZAIAH: "Don't worry. I'll stay here with him. You guys go ahead."

So Helicopter Jim, Mr. Cape, Scott, and Princess Eva headed toward the area where they thought the Cave of Faith was. As they're heading across the river, the water begins to bubble up even more. They're almost to the other side and all of a sudden, Mikhail opens his eyes...

AND THAT WILL BE THE NEXT ADVENTURE OF HELICOPTER JIM.

Adventure 147

On the last adventure of Helicopter Jim, as they were crossing Diamond River, to find the Cave of Faith, Mikhail senses something. He stands in the middle of the river with his eyes closed.

MR. CAPE: "Jim, something is definitely wrong. We need to get to the cave quickly."

HJ: "But what do we do with Mikhail? He's just standing there."

MR. CAPE: "He'll be fine."

ZAIAH: "Don't worry. I'll stay here with him. You guys go ahead."

So Helicopter Jim, Mr. Cape, Scott, and Princess Eva headed toward the area where they thought the Cave of Faith was. As they're heading across the river, the water begins to bubble up even more. They're almost to the other side and all of a sudden, Mikhail opens his eyes…

AND NOW WE BEGIN THE ADVENTURES OF HELICOPTER JIM!

MIKHAIL: "Dayor is here!"

HJ: "What do you mean, Dayor is here?"

SCOTT: "Dayor? Wha...what do you mean? Where...where is he exactly?"

MIKHAIL: "He's here. I sense that he's here. I know he's nearby. That much I can tell you."

Just then Mikhail sees movement on the top of the highest waterfall. And as he looks, he sees more and more of Dayor's army come forward. At the tops of all of these waterfalls, Dayor's army begins surrounding them all.

HJ: "What is it Mikhail?"

MIKHAIL: "We are surrounded by Dayor's army."

And sure enough, Dayor shows up. Dayor is at the top of the waterfall. And he calls out to Jim...

DAYOR: "Jim, finally, we meet again. But this time you will not be successful. This time I will end it all and I will have the Stones. And I will destroy you."

HJ: "Mikhail, what do we do? What do we do? Do we go to the Cave of Faith? Do we... do we see the Seer? I mean, go to the Seer? What do we do?"

MIKHAIL: "It's your call, Jim. What do you want to do?"

HJ: "I don't know."

So Helicopter Jim takes out January and he uses strength of the mind and he uses wisdom. Wisdom says to stand their ground and go into battle. So Helicopter Jim says to everyone...

HJ: "Hey guys, I know the Cave of Faith is right there, and Dayor and his armies are right here. But I...I...I don't think we can... I don't think we can... we can get away this time. I think we need to stand our ground. Otherwise, we'll be running for a long time."

SCOTT: "Jim, whatever you want to do, I'm with you." And everyone else agreed.

HJ: "Okay, we armor up. Let's do this."

Helicopter Jim addressed Dayor...

HJ: (SPEAKING TO DAYOR ATOP THE WATERFALL) "Dayor, these Stones do not belong to you. There is a reason why we need to return these Stones to its birthplace. We need peace in the universe. Everyone needs peace."

DAYOR: "No! Just because you say we need peace doesn't mean we need peace. Your peace is not like my peace. I want things differently. Therefore, you are going to have to pay the consequences and suffer the consequences for not giving me the Stones."

Dayor lifted up his hands and he commanded water creatures to come up from under where Jim and the rest of the team were. And as the waters continue to boil, all of these water creatures came out. They looked weird...many of them were massive creatures that they had never seen before.

HJ: "I guess we are battling these guys. Let's back each other up. And let's make sure that we come out victorious."

Helicopter Jim gives Zaiah the Stone of August.

HJ: "Zaiah hang on to this and make sure that no one is hurt. You are able to turn invisible. Scott, you stay by my side. Princess Eva, you and Mr. Cape team-up. Mikhail, you know what to do. (HELICOPTER NAME) get in position. And Blue... fly high and let it rain!"

Blue let out a loud shriek and shot up...way into the sky (EAGLE SHRIEK). Dayor looked at Blue and was in shock. He did not know that Helicopter Jim was able to bring Blue to life.

DAYOR: "What is Blue doing here?!"

And so all the water creatures were coming out and attacking Jim and the rest of the team. Scott and Helicopter Jim put on the Final Cloak and they both camouflaged, no one could see them. Scott used his InvisiBow and was able to take out creature after creature. Helicopter Jim used Legendary, the nuke sword and he was able to take down creature after creature, large and small.

He used little spikes on one of the creatures that looked like a snake.

SCOTT: "Jim, what in the world is that?"

HJ: "I have no idea. That thing is gross."

SCOTT: "I know. There's like, slime all over the place. That...that is gross."

Mr. Cape used the UnbreakaBow and he shot arrow after arrow and was able to control the arrows to hit different creatures. Zaiah made sure everyone was protected using his Power Sword. Just then, Dayor released even more creatures. Some of the creatures had unbelievable powers.

Helicopter Jim was becoming weak and tired. Princess Eva was using the Ring of Protection and she was not damaged at all. She also was using the Never-Ending Chain. And as she continued to do damage to all the different creatures that attacked her, more creatures began to surround her...there were so many...she was outnumbered. It was time... So she called out to Zaiah.

PRINCESS EVA: "Zaiah! Bring me Destiny."

ZAIAH: "My pleasure Princess!"

Zaiah takes out the Sword of Destiny and tosses it to Princess Eva. She wasn't able to see, but right behind her, one of the creatures was just about to attack her, when all of a sudden, a massive ball of ice smashes the creature... just before it hurt Princess Eva.

Princess Eva turns around and looks up... and it was Blue. Blue shot a ball of ice.

PRINCESS EVA: "Thanks, big fella!"

BLUE: (EAGLE SHRIEK)

The creature was still alive. Princess Eva used Destiny and took out the creature. Another creature from the water attacks Princess Eva. She ducked and used Destiny to destroy that creature. Mr. Cape continued to protect Helicopter Jim and Scott with his UnbreakaBow, but more and more creatures were surrounding them. Helicopter Jim was getting tired and as more and more creatures surround them, Blue continues to bring down ice ball after ice ball.

Helicopter Jim is using Little Spikes and he's taking out creatures but there are so many of them. They don't know what to do. Mikhail takes the Power Staff and strikes the ground (BRGSHHHH!) and he wipes out almost all of the creatures. Dayor once again, instructs more of the creatures to come up out of the water…

HJ: "Mikhail, this is not working! There are too many creatures coming out. We need to head up to the top. We need to get to Dayor!"

And so Helicopter Jim calls Blue and Blue comes down.

HJ: "Everybody, get on."

AND THAT WILL BE THE NEXT ADVENTURE OF HELICOPTER JIM.

Adventure 148

On the last adventure of Helicopter Jim, they are battling all of the creatures that Dayor called up from Diamond River, but it's very difficult to defeat them all.

Helicopter Jim is using Little Spikes and he's taking out creatures but there are so many of them. They don't know what to do. Mikhail takes the Power Staff and strikes the ground (BRGSHHHH!) and he wipes out almost all of the creatures. Dayor once again, instructs more of the creatures to come up out of the water…

HJ: "Mikhail, this is not working! There are too many creatures coming out. We need to head up to the top. We need to get to Dayor!"

And so Helicopter Jim calls Blue and Blue comes down.

HJ: "Everybody, get on."

AND NOW WE BEGIN THE ADVENTURES OF HELICOPTER JIM!

And as they got on, Helicopter Jim instructed (HELICOPTER NAME) to meet them at the top.

And so (HELICOPTER NAME) went up and so did Helicopter Jim. And as they're on the top of the waterfall, they are on one side and Dayor is on the other side.

HJ: "(HELICOPTER NAME) you're going to have to unleash a lot of your weaponry and we're going to have to take out Dayor."

HELICOPTER: "Whatever you need me to do Jim, I'm right

here."

HJ: "Do what you need to do and let's attack him all at once. And we're high enough, that the creatures cannot get to us. They have to stay on the ground...near the water. I noticed that every time we injured them, they turned and headed into the water. So they need water for strength and healing...and being up here, they're not able to attack us. Guys... we're going to have to do this together."

MR. CAPE: (CONCERNED) "But Jim, we're growing weaker by the minute!"

HJ: "I know, I know... wait... (PAUSE) we have July!"

Helicopter Jim takes out the Stone of July and he brings everyone together and uses the Stone of July to give everyone else increased physical strength. All of a sudden, everyone was empowered even more and they were strengthened more than what they ever had.

SCOTT: (FLEXING HIS MUSCLES) "Oh my goodness, this thing is incredible! I...I...I can definitely feel the strength! Wow, look at these arms!"

PRINCESS EVA: "Yes, I feel it too! Scott..."

SCOTT: "What's up?"

PRINCESS EVA: "Sorry to tell you...but your arms..."

SCOTT: "Yea?"

PRINCESS EVA: "They're the same size."

SCOTT: (UNDER HIS BREATH AND FEELING HIS ARMS) "Looks bigger to me."

MIKHAIL: "I think we all feel stronger!"

ZAIAH: "I, even I can feel that power. It's this...this is a strength I've never felt before."

HJ: "Well then, let's go! Blue, take us to the other side. Let's get Dayor!"

As they head to the other side…

HJ: "(HELICOPTER NAME) hit him with Sonic Lightning!"

HELICOPTER: "You got it!"

(HELICOPTER NAME) hit Dayor with Sonic Lightning.

HJ: "Blue, give them a ball of ice!"

And so Blue gave a loud cry (EAGLE CRY) and shot off a massive ball of ice. Sonic Lightning and a ball of ice was able to hit Dayor and there was a massive water cloud as a result.

Because of the ball of ice, as they got closer, Helicopter Jim tried to see where Dayor was, but he had a hard time seeing because of the cloud that surrounded him, the cloud that surrounded Dayor. So he couldn't see what was happening.

HJ: "(HELICOPTER NAME) can you, can you scan and see if we took him out?"

HELICOPTER: "He's not even there."

HJ: "What do you mean he's not there? Did we destroy him? Did we take him out?"

HELICOPTER: "No, he's not there at all."

Just then the sky became dark. Clouds started to form…

HJ: "What is, what is going on? This is, this is weird."

MIKHAIL: "This *is* very weird."

SCOTT: "Okay, what...what is weird? You're talking about the weather or weird that, uh, we just attacked Dayor and he's...he's not even there. What... I don't get it. What is, what is weird about what is happening?"

MIKHAIL: "No, the clouds that are forming. This is not a good sign."

PRINCESS EVA: "You know what I find weird, is the armies of Dayor did not even attack or move. Something definitely is...is wrong."

HJ: "Yeah, I...I found, I found that kind of odd too."

MR. CAPE: "Hey guys, I hate to tell you this, but we are in one of Dayor's mind wars."

HJ: "What do you mean? What is that...a mind war?"

MR. CAPE: "Dayor is very powerful. Right now, we're not fighting against Dayor. We're fighting against Dayor's mind. He is controlling everything right now."

HJ: "Then...okay. So how do we, how do we, how do we win this thing?"

MR. CAPE: "We don't. We're just going to have to go through the battle or we head to the Cave of Faith. Either way, we're going to have to make a move. These clouds that are forming are being controlled by Dayor."

HJ: "Well, I say we go to the Cave of Faith."

MIKHAIL: "Jim, I think we're too late."

HJ: "What do you mean we're too late? Why are we too late?"

MIKHAIL: "Look down there."

And when they looked down below, the armies of Dayor were blocking the area where the Cave of Faith was.

HJ: "Well, we're just going to have to go through them."

All of a sudden Helicopter Jim hears something behind them.

HELICOPTER: "Jim, lookout!"

Jim turns around and a massive dark cloud hits him so hard that he's knocked off of the cliff and is heading towards the bottom where the waterfalls are. Blue is also startled because of the hit. Helicopter Jim is falling. At the same time, what Jim didn't know is that when he got hit, all of the Stones flew out of his pouch and Jim is trying to catch the Stones that are falling in midair.

HJ: (AS HE'S FALLING) "Nooooo! The Stones! C'mon!"

Jim is doing his best to capture the Stones as he's falling and as each Stone is heading in different directions, he is able to catch May, August, July...then June... all of the Stones except for January and February. And as he's falling January and February drop into one of the largest waterfalls. As Jim is falling, Blue comes down and catches Jim…

HJ: "Blue, the Stones! We can't... how do we get the Stones?"

MIKHAIL: "Jim, you just gotta let it go. You can't get it.

That's too dangerous. We can't go down there and get it."

HJ: "Then what do we do? How do we get those Stones?"

SCOTT: "Jim, we, I don't know how we're gonna-- The only way we can get it is... remember the Stone of October? For some reason, it just says the Stone of October is the one that is able to locate the Stones, right...that we once possessed, but have since lost? We don't know where they went. Yes we can go down there and look for them, but do you know how dangerous that is? We can't just go down there and... and... uh, and... and go under the water. Do you know how powerful that, that waterfall is?"

AND THAT WILL BE THE NEXT ADVENTURE OF HELICOPTER JIM.

Adventure 149

On the last adventure of Helicopter Jim, Jim, Scott, Mikhail, Princess Eva, Mr. Cape, Zaiah, Blue and (HELICOPTER NAME), are doing their best to defeat Dayor, but find themselves in a battle in Dayor's mind.

Jim uses July to strengthen everyone...but by then, Dayor's army is blocking the area where the Cave of Faith is. As they prepare themselves, Helicopter Jim unexpectedly gets hit by a massive dark cloud. It hits him so hard that he's knocked off of the cliff and is heading towards the bottom where the waterfalls are.

When he got hit, all of the Stones flew out of his pouch, and he lost January and February somewhere in the waterfall. All the other Stones, he was able to catch.

Jim is falling towards the bottom of the waterfall...and right before Jim plunges into the water below, Blue catches Jim...

HJ: "Blue, the Stones! We can't... how do we get the Stones?"

MIKHAIL: "Jim, you just gotta let it go. You can't get it. That's too dangerous. We can't go down there and get it."

HJ: "Then what do we do? How do we get the Stones?"

SCOTT: "Jim, we, I don't know how we're gonna-- The only way we can get it is... remember the Stone of October? For some reason, it just says the Stone of October is the one that is able to locate the Stones, right...that we once possessed, but have since lost? We don't know where they went. Yes we can go down there and look for them, but do you know how dangerous that is? We can't just go down there and... and... uh, and... and go under the water. Do you know how powerful that, that waterfall is?"

AND NOW WE BEGIN THE ADVENTURES OF HELICOPTER JIM!

So Helicopter Jim and the rest of the team knew that they could not go down there and retrieve January and February. The rest of Dayor's army was still there and Helicopter Jim didn't know what to do. Jim enters (HELICOPTER NAME)...

HJ: (BREATHING HEAVILY) "Dad, did you hear.. just, did you hear what just happened? I lost some of the Stones and... and Dayor's army is here and I don't know what to do."

JS: "Jim, you know what to do. You just have to do what you *need* to do."

HJ: "(HELICOPTER NAME), you're gonna have to take out those guys down there with whatever weaponry you have."

HELICOPTER: "What do you need me to do?"

HJ: "Hit him with Sonic Lightning."

So (HELICOPTER NAME) did that. He hit them with Sonic Lightning but nothing happened.

HJ: "Why didn't it work? How could it not work? Why, why didn't they get injured? How can they just be standing there?"

ZAIAH: "Jim, what, what does that Sonic Lightning do?"

HJ: "It's supposed to paralyze them. It... it... it... it disrupts their nervous system."

PRINCESS EVA: "But they're... but they're not... they're not... they're not damaged by it. That doesn't make sense then if that... if it was supposed to do that."

HELICOPTER: "Jim, you're not going to believe this, but all that we've been seeing, all of the armies...they're not even here. I can see them, but it's as if they're not there. They don't exist here."

MR. CAPE: "Jim, I told you, this is Dayor's war of the mind. In other words, Dayor is projecting these things. They're not even there, we're fighting a battle that doesn't even exist, Dayor is doing all of this with his mind. Dayor isn't even here."

HJ: "What? So that means we can go to the Cave of Faith?"

MR. CAPE: "I believe so."

MIKHAIL: "That makes sense because I didn't... I wasn't sensing that there was danger. I was sensing that there was confusion and whatever Dayor is up to, it's not going to be good. We need to get out of here. It's getting darker and darker. We need to get to the Cave of Faith… now!"

HJ: "But what do we do about the Stones?"

MIKHAIL: "Jim, where are we going to go? We can't... look down there... look at all of that... the water... and how it's so powerful."

PRINCESS EVA: "You know Jim, under that waterfall... all of these waterfalls... are so many different tunnels and... and caves under there. The Stones can be anywhere in the land right now because this area feeds the entire surrounding region. The entire world of Diamond Crust is connected to these waterfalls.

So the Stones could be anywhere by now."

HJ: "But I need to get the Stones. It's my responsibility. I can't lose the Stones."

SCOTT: "Jim, it's okay. We...we will figure out a way."

HJ: (UPSET) "It's not okay Scott! It's not okay. It's not easy to get these Stones. It's not easy at all!"

SCOTT: "I know it's not easy! It's... I know it's very difficult. It's difficult for all of us!"

HJ: (ANGRY AND EMOTIONAL) "It's not difficult for all of us. It's difficult for *me*! You don't know what it's like to carry this burden. You don't know what it's like for me to... to have to risk my life to get these Stones."

MR. CAPE: "Hey Jim, just calm down a bit."

HJ: "What do you mean calm down? We've worked so hard to get these Stones. I'm not going to just let it disappear in front of us."

JS: "You know Jim, you're right... but so is Mr. Cape, and so is Scott. You guys have been doing this together. I agree with them Jim, just let it go for now. Go to the Seer and see what he says."

HJ: (TAKE A BREATH AND PAUSE) "I'm sorry Scott. I'm sorry. I'm sorry I got upset. Dad, you're right. Let's go to the Cave of Faith. Let's... let's... let's go from here. Scott, I'm so sorry."

SCOTT: "It's okay Jim. It was a very intense day. Intense battle, intense... intense everything... and... we're okay Jim. We're good."

HJ: "Okay guys, let's just go to the Cave of Faith. Let's go to the Seer and see what he says."

And so they headed to the Cave of Faith. They were able to go through the Cave of Faith and as they did, they got to the other side and were able to speak to the Seer.

AND THAT WILL BE THE NEXT ADVENTURE OF HELICOPTER JIM.

Adventure 150

On the last adventure of Helicopter Jim, they all found out that the battle they've been fighting was a battle of Dayor's mind. Jim was so upset that he lost January and February that his anger got the best of him.

MR. CAPE: "Hey Jim, just calm down a bit."

HJ: "What do you mean calm down? We've worked so hard to get these Stones. I'm not going to just let it disappear in front of us."

JS: "You know Jim, you're right... but so is Mr. Cape, and so is Scott. You guys have been doing this together. I agree with them Jim, just let it go for now. Go to the Seer and see what he says."

HJ: (TAKE A BREATHE AND PAUSE) "I'm sorry Scott. I'm sorry. I'm sorry I got upset. Dad, you're right. Let's go to the Cave of Faith. Let's... let's... let's go from here. Scott, I'm so sorry."

SCOTT: "It's okay Jim. It was a very intense day. Intense battle, intense... intense everything... and... we're okay Jim. We're good."

HJ: "Okay guys, let's just go to the Cave of Faith. Let's go to the Seer and see what he says."

And so they headed to the Cave of Faith. They were able to go through the Cave of Faith and as they did, they got to the other side and were able to speak to the Seer.

AND NOW WE BEGIN THE ADVENTURES OF

HELICOPTER JIM!

SEER: "Welcome back Jim."

HJ: "Well it's good to see you...I have...I have so many questions...and I could be here forever...but, I will have to wait for another time to answer those questions."

SEER: "So what brings you here today? What is so pressing that you need answers right away?

HJ: (EMBARRASSED) "Long story short... I lost two stones in the massive waterfalls and I have no idea where they are...but... that's not the point. Well that's kind of the point...what I'm trying to say is, *I need October,* and I have no clue of where to begin!"

SEER: "Well... you know that October is fiery orange in color..."

HJ. "Yes, well we know that...?"

SCOTT: "Yeah we got that... we know...we know what color it is... we just don't know *where* it is. So can you tell us where it is? It'll make things a lot easier and a lot safer... *and* quicker for us to carry out Jim's mission."

SEER: "Well, it's not that simple. As I said before, I don't know exactly where the Stones are located, and even if I did know, you still would have to retrieve it."

SCOTT: (IRRITATED) "Yeah, yeah, yeah, *but,* it would save us a lot of time if you knew where they were."

SEER: "Well... I can't help you there. What I can tell you...which is what you already know... is that the Stone of

October is fiery orange in color. My guess is that it might be in a place where there's a lot of fire. And the only place that I can think of that has a lot of fire, is on Magmatia. "

HJ: "Okay...no...you see... that's the one place I was dreading! Because on Magmatia, isn't it... isn't it loaded with...covered with... volcanoes and lava and all of that!?"

SEER: "Yes... but not the entire world of it."

PRINCESS EVA: "Jim, why don't we just go to Magmatia? We... we know we need to get the Stones anyway and while we're on Magmatia we might as well get April."

MR. CAPE: "That's... that sounds great to me. We are gonna need October and you don't want time to go by because the more time that goes by, the harder it is, and the harder it will be to find January and February. The current will push those Stones practically anywhere it could even be underground... we don't know. But we need October."

ZAIAH: "I agree, I say let's go to Magmatia."

PRINCESS EVA: "Jim no matter what you decide, we're with you 100%."

MIKHAIL: "Yes we are... I am with you Jim... whatever you decide."

SCOTT: "I'm with you... whatever you decide Jim... I mean... we're gonna have to go to Magmatia... sometime. There's never a good time to go to Magmatia anyway... so, we might as well just go."

HJ: "True. Well, thank you so much... we really appreciate all your wisdom and we hope that when we get to Magmatia, we will be able to locate October."

So Helicopter Jim and the entire team headed to the Western Jump Cave where they were transported to Magmatia.

(TRANSPORT SOUND F/X)

ZAIAH: "Wow that was weird. Okay, so, now that we're here, we need to find the Stone of October...so where do we start Jim?"

HJ: "Well I wasn't given (HELICOPTER NAME) for nothing. (HELICOPTER NAME), can you scan the area... just to see what you come up with?"

And so (HELICOPTER NAME) scanned the entire area.

HELICOPTER: "Well I can tell you this, this place is filled with lava. There are areas you can go to, and there are lava tubes that you can go into, but this entire region, has lava everywhere."

SCOTT: "What?! The Seer was wrong?! The Seer said that the whole place isn't filled with lava."

HJ: "Well the Seer is correct, the entire place isn't filled with lava. There are places you can go to, we just need to map it out."

MIKHAIL: "Let me get a lay of the land."

And so they stepped out of the cave and as they did, right in front of them, was an entire area of molten lava, like an ocean of lava. With a large city in the middle of it in the far distance.

SCOTT: (POINTING) "That...that...that better not be the place we need to go to.

MR. CAPE: "Scott…(TAKE DEEP BREATH AND SIGH) I

believe it is."

HELICOPTER: "Jim... that's the first place we need to go to."

And so they all jumped into (HELICOPTER NAME) and flew pretty high up and made their way towards this huge city that was located in the middle of this ocean of lava.

HJ: "You know... this reminds me of Lava City. I mean... but the difference is... like, this whole city is surrounded by an ocean of lava! Look at how massive the city is! How do they get in... and...and how do they go out?"

And as they got closer, they could see all of the people down below. And so as they approach, as they get closer to the city...Helicopter Jim could see that at the top of the city, was this massive Palace, and the Palace looked like it was made out of liquid lava. It looked hardened, yet still liquefied.

AND THAT WILL BE THE NEXT ADVENTURE OF HELICOPTER JIM!

Made in the USA
Middletown, DE
27 March 2022